"You should always wear your hair like this . . ."

His breath was warm on her lips. "You look like my wood nymph again . . . Jane." Then he was kissing her, slowly and gently at first, his lips as soft and sweet as she could ever hope for, while his fingers stroked her neck and shoulders lightly beneath the collar of her dressing gown. Then it wasn't gentle at all; she was pulled hard against him, and for a moment she struggled in the face of a force and a rush of desire that she did not understand. But it was useless to struggle and soon she had no wish to struggle anyway. She wrapped her arms around his neck, allowing her lips to open under his, tasting the sweetness of his mouth, drowning in her longing for him. His hand pulled at the belt of her dressing gown and it fell open so that only the double layer of nylon was between her soft skin and his hands. . . .

Bantam Circle of Love Romances
Ask your bookseller for the books you have missed

1 GOLD IN HER HAIR by Anne Neville
2 ROYAL WEDDING by Mary Christopher
3 GATES OF THE SUN by Lucinda Day
4 DESIGN FOR ENCHANTMENT
   by Rachel Murray
5 THE CINDERELLA SEASON
   by Elaine Daniel
6 ASHTON'S FOLLY by Jean Innes
7 A RING AT THE READY by Anna West
8 THE RELUCTANT DAWN
   by Juliet Lawrence
9 THE HEATHER IS WINDBLOWN
   by Anne Saunders
10 VOICES OF LOVING by Anne Neville
11 MIDSUMMER DREAMS by Amalia James
12 LOVE'S DREAM by Christine Baker
13 THREAD OF SCARLET by Rachel Murray
14 THE BOTTICELLI MAN
   by Alexandra Blakelee
15 HERON'S KEEP by Samantha Clare

Dear Friend,

Enter the Circle of Love — and travel to faraway places with romantic heroes . . .

We read hundreds of novels and, each month, select the very best — from the finest writers around the world — to bring you these wonderful love stories . . . stories that let *you* share in a variety of beautiful romantic experiences.

With Circle of Love Romances, you treat yourself to a romantic holiday — anytime, anywhere. And because we want to please you, won't you write and let us know your comments and suggestions?

Meanwhile, welcome to the Circle of Love — we don't think you'll ever want to leave!

Best,

Cathy Camhy
Editor

CIRCLE OF LOVE™

Voices of
Loving

by Anne Neville

BANTAM BOOKS
TORONTO · NEW YORK · LONDON · SYDNEY

For Bob

VOICES OF LOVING

*A Bantam Book/published by arrangement with
Robert Hale, Ltd.*

PRINTING HISTORY

First published in Great Britain 1978.

*Circle of Love, the garland and the ring designs are
trademarks of Bantam Books, Inc.*

Bantam edition/May 1982

ISBN 0-553-21538-8

Published simultaneously in the United States and Canada

PRINTED IN THE UNITED STATES OF AMERICA

0 9 8 7 6 5 4 3 2 1

Voices of
Loving

One

It was raining that particular morning that Jane walked into the offices of Emerson, Emerson and Marks, the firm of solicitors for whom she had worked for two years. England had revelled in a glorious summer but now it was October and a dismal, dull autumn soon caused everyone to forget the long hot days of July and August. Perhaps her mood merely reflected the weather, Jane thought, as she shook out her wet raincoat and hung it up. She felt wet and cold, dreary and depressed, at least ten years older than her twenty-three years.

With the exception of the senior, Miss Spencer, all the girls Jane worked with were younger than herself. Miss Spencer was in her early fifties, a confirmed spinster who lived for her budgy, her poodle and Emerson, Emerson and Marks. Apart from her and Jane, the turnover of staff was rapid; the girls seemed to be uniformly pretty and gay, and were snapped up into marriage in no time. Even though Jane was sure there was more to life than simply getting married, it did at times get very depressing.

Today was the turn of a girl called Margaret, who had left school only six months earlier. Jane

admired her small solitaire diamond engagement ring, set about organising the usual collec-
tion, and wondered gloomily whether, in twenty
years time, the girls would talk about "Poor Miss
Murray" as they now talked of "Poor Miss Spencer." She took out her dissatisfaction on her
typewriter and thought about throwing in this
miserable, boring job and looking for something
more exciting. But what? She borrowed Miss
Spencer's copy of the Daily Telegraph and
scanned the Situations Vacant pages, but there
were no marvellous ads calling for a "young
female to act as companion to rich lady on World
Cruise" or "Assistant for wealthy, world famous
novelist in the Caribbean." Even if there had been,
Jane reflected, it wasn't likely she would be
chosen for anything so exciting. She was altogether too ordinary for anyone to want as a
companion or personal assistant. It wasn't that
she was bad looking, she decided, going into the
rest room at the beginning of the lunch hour and
peering critically at herself in the mirror. She had
very pale hair that her father used to say was the
colour of moon beams, very long, fine hair it was,
too straight and fine to be worn loose in the office,
and generally confined in a rather severe chignon. Her eyes, almost too large for her small, pale
face, were very dark brown, unusual enough in
contrast to the silver blonde hair to be called
striking-almost! If only, she thought sadly, she
didn't look so waif-like, or so depressingly young.
Not gay-young like Margaret and the other girls,
but school girlish. And if she applied more make
up than just a touch of lipstick, she looked like a
child who had got at its mother's make-up bag.

"Oh, blow it!" she muttered at her reflection,
and grabbed her raincoat, heading out of the

office. Usually her lunch consisted of a cup of coffee and a sandwich in a café across the road; usually she ate alone. Today, just as she reached street level, her name was called and Margaret came bounding down the stairs, long hair flapping, full of youthful enthusiasm.

"Oh, Jane, thank goodness I caught you!" she gasped, before she had even reached the bottom stair. "I've got a message for you. I was so excited today that I forgot everything else. It came while you were in Mr. Emerson's office." She held out a piece of paper, reading the words aloud. "A man called Alistair Bennett phoned. Could you meet him at twelve-thirty at the Silver Peacock?" She looked up at Jane. "Anything wrong? I didn't say you'd definitely be there so you needn't . . . you've gone awfully pale."

Jane swallowed hard and shook her head stiffly, making an effort to pull her thoughts into order. She managed a weak smile for Margaret's benefit. "No, there's nothing wrong. It was a bit of a shock, that's all. I haven't heard anything of Alistair for years."

"Oh?" Margaret grinned. "An old flame?"

Was Alistair that? Jane wondered, giving a non-committal smile and leaving Margaret wondering. He had taken her out off and on for over a year and she had fallen heavily for him. He was a good bit older than herself—about fifteen years she guessed—and in all fairness to him, he had never tried to hide the fact that he continued to take other women out, many of them more sophisticated and older than Jane had been. There were several of them, for Alistair was good looking, charming and interesting, the sort of man who could make a girl feel cherished and special. Jane had never blamed him because she fell in love with him, but she had been only eighteen when they met, eighteen and frighteningly naïve and, looking back over the last five years, she felt that he could have been more careful of her feelings. He couldn't possibly have been unaware of what she felt for him.

Jane thought of all this as she walked to the Silver Peacock—it was typical of Alistair's arrogance that he had chosen this place, where they had so often met in the past. Memories crowded in on her—his cool, sweet kisses, his tender embraces, always gentle and guaranteed not to frighten even the green girl that Jane Murray had been in those days. She wondered if it was fair to blame Alistair for the unexciting state of her life these days; when he had gone off suddenly and got himself married, she had thought herself finished with men. Men, she had believed with the intolerance of youth that allows no shades of grey, were cruel and faithless and she wanted no part of them. Such ideas can become habit forming and though now she was older and more capable of coping with any unwanted masculine advances, she still tended to shy away from emotional entanglements.

Yet here she was running swiftly the moment Alistair called. Curiosity perhaps? Or did she . . . was it possible that she still felt for him as she had four years ago? Or was she merely "laying a ghost"? Jane didn't know. What she did know was that she had to see Alistair and find out what he wanted.

The Silver Peacock was a restaurant, very "olde worlde" downstairs, with oak furniture, chintz curtains and beautiful fifteenth century panelling, where the old ladies of Brampton sipped china tea and ate cream cakes in the afternoons; very chic and modern upstairs. There was a bar adjacent to the upstairs restaurant and it was here that Jane found Alistair. She scarcely had time to do more than recognise him before she was being hugged and kissed, held at arms' length and told she hadn't changed a bit.

And he was the same Alistair. Dressed in a sheepskin jacket over a yellow polo neck sweater and brown corded slacks, he looked expensive and country squirish. It seemed to Jane though that there was a harder look in his hazel eyes and little lines were etched round his mouth that hadn't been there before.

"What'll it be? The usual?" he asked gaily.

"I don't know. What was the usual?" Jane inquired lightly, but with an underlying dryness that caused him to glance sharply at her as though he had suddenly realised she might not be the rather malleable creature she once had been.

"You used to drink sweet sherry."

"Did I? But then, I was only nineteen at the time. I usually drink whisky now, but as I have to go back to work, I'll have a lager, please."

He ordered the lager and another gin for himself, and they sat in one of the small, intimate alcoves where they could also eat. Jane said that she hadn't very long, so he set about ordering lunch immediately. As he spoke to the waiter, Jane watched him, feeling curiously detached and even a trifle light headed. It was strange to sit there so close to him, knowing that she no longer felt anything for him. To her now, he looked what she supposed he had always been, a sharp, ruthless man who would stop at nothing to

5

achieve his ambitions. She wondered why he wanted to see her and was conscious of curiosity about his movements over the last few years.

"Are you still with *Women's Life?*" she asked, referring to the women's magazine of which he had been features editor when she first knew him. He was eating pâté and chewed absently on a piece of toast as he shook his head.

"Ever heard of *Looking Glass?*"

"Of course. Who hasn't?"

Looking Glass was a new magazine that had erupted on to the market some seven or eight months ago. Most of the girls Jane worked with bought it and wasted many hours discussing the articles and features in it. It was aimed at women between the ages of about twenty and thirty-five and was very pro Women's Lib.

"What do you think of it?" Alistair asked.

Jane shrugged. She didn't go much on Women's Lib herself and personally thought the ideas expressed in *Looking Glass* were a little too free and easy, giving the direct impression that promiscuity was a desirable state of affairs. Jane was aware that to many people her ideas on the subject were extremely outdated, and was diffident enough to keep them to herself.

"I've only glanced through it a couple of times," she said evasively. "I don't read magazines much."

"I forgot. You always have a damn great classic on the go—Dickens, Tolstoy or Scott." He sounded amused, as though he were humouring her, but Jane made no comment as the waiter chose that moment to bring over the main course. Alistair had ordered grouse but Jane's choice had been a light salad as she was unaccustomed to eating much at midday. In a moment Alistair continued speaking, saying proudly, "I own *Looking Glass*." Jane supposed her surprise must have shown for he continued, "I started it up in a partnership but I bought my partner out in August. The magazine is doing well, very well indeed. We have a reputation for getting big, outspoken articles about celebrities—film stars, pop singers, sports personalities, politicians. The sort of features the bigger, better known magazines can't get."

Jane nodded. One of the copies of *Looking Glass* she had glanced at, contained a near libellous account of the life of a female American singer who led a riot of a life. If every edition was as hot, no wonder it was doing well. Alistair talked on about the magazine while Jane wondered yet again what she was doing there. Surely Alistair hadn't invited her there just so that he could blow his own trumpet. They went back to the bar where Jane had coffee and he another gin, and she told him she had to go back to work. Only then did he start getting anywhere near the point.

"Look, Jane, I realise I haven't mentioned why I wanted to see you. The thing is, it's complicated and a bit dicey and this is no place to talk. I'm going back to London on Saturday but meantime I've loaned one of those new apartments out on the Lower Road. You know where I mean? Could you come round this evening, straight after work, and let me explain? It's on your bus route and naturally I'll run you home afterwards."

"Well . . . I don't know," Jane hesitated uncertainly. "What about your wife?"

"My wife?" He looked pained. "I thought you would have heard. We were divorced last year."

"No, I didn't know. I'm sorry." Strange that if she had heard about it then, she would probably have lived in hope that he might one day turn back to her. Now she just didn't care.

"Will you come round?" Alistair prompted urgently. "I really think you will be interested in the proposition I have to put to you. Do you find your present job interesting?"

Jane smiled a little. "Not especially," she admitted.

"In that case, I'll give you a small clue, as a sort of mouth waterer. I'm offering you the chance to put a little excitement into your life. Oh, not—" he added hastily, "on a personal level. I realise you and I have grown away from each other over the last four years. But this will be—let's say to our mutual advantage."

After that, Jane could hardly refuse to listen to him. After all, she had only been thinking that morning how boring her life was, and what a rut she was sinking into. "I could do with a bit of excitement," she admitted seriously, to Alistair, and he told her how to reach his apartment before they parted.

The apartment, which belonged to one of Alistair's London friends, was the residence of a rich man. It was ultra modern, contemporarily furnished and decorated in oranges, greens, blues and yellows, a horrible combination that caused Jane to shudder, though she guessed the interior decoration had probably cost a small fortune. Alistair greeted her with a hearty handshake and a kiss that she was not quick enough to avoid. He poured her a whisky and indicated a chair, an uncomfortable looking contraption of canvas and chrome that proved to be remarkably comfortable once she had wriggled about in it for a few seconds.

"I'll get straight to the point," Alistair said, standing in front of her, a large gin in his hand. "How are your typing and shorthand? Up to scratch?"

This was the last thing Jane had expected, but she nodded. "I could hardly hold down my job otherwise, could I? Why do you want to know?"

He didn't answer at once. He lit a cigar and offered her a cigarette box. Jane shook her head absently. "I suppose you're too young to have heard of Max Carstairs," he said.

In that statement he couldn't have been more wrong. Jane didn't see the connection between her typing ability and Max Carstairs but in one blinding flash of recall she was back in the Shakespeare Memorial theatre at Stratford on Avon, a thin, earnest ten-year-old who sat in rapt delight beside her father, staring unblinkingly at the stage as the drama of "Henry V" was enacted before her. James Murray had been a devotee of Shakespeare and brought up his only daughter with a similar passion. He delighted to take her to the theatre and the Stratford trip was a tenth birthday treat. Jane remembered it as one of the loveliest days of her life; after the play they had dined in style at an expensive restaurant and she wore a long dress, her first, and he a dinner jacket.

"I saw him as Henry V at Stratford," she said softly. "Thirteen years ago. He was wonderful." The words were wholly inadequate; how could mere words describe how it had felt to listen to that beautiful voice speaking the empassioned, familiar words? Or to see Max Carstairs, tall and slender and straight, dark hair cropped short, splendid in the vivid, colourful costumes of the period. "Of course, I've seen the two films he made too."

"That's right. *Antony and Cleopatra* and *Jane Eyre*. Carstairs must be almost forty now. No longer acting of course."

"Oh, yes. Wasn't there something about a car crash? I seem to remember reading about it. A couple of years ago?"

"Four years actually," Alistair nodded. "I've got a dossier with all the relevant information. You can read it later. The thing is, since he gave up the stage, Carstairs has embarked on a very different career, equally successful in its own way. He writes thrillers, under the name of Michael Collins. Ring a bell?"

"I'll say!" Jane enthused. "I've read a couple of them. Real top class thrillers very well researched. The last one, about the air crash over the Alps, was a real cliff hanger. Imagine Michael Collins really being Max Carstairs." She frowned a little as she remembered what the actor looked like the last time she saw him, as Mr. Rochester in *Jane Eyre*; vague memories of a tall, broad-shouldered man, really too good looking to be Rochester, came back to her. That, of course, had been seven or eight years ago. There had been an innate sensitivity about Carstairs the actor, a sensitivity noticeably lacking in the novels he wrote, stories with all the necessary ingredients for success these days; sex, violence and tension, all linked together by really good plots.

"What has all this to do with me?" Jane asked.

Alistair reached for a thick box file on the table beside him and handed it to her. "I'll leave you to glance through this lot," he told her. "I've some phone calls to make."

The file contained mainly photostat copies of newspaper and magazine articles about Max Carstairs. There were theatre bills, all with his name on the cast list, generally at the top; then there were clippings about the two films he had made and an assortment of black and white stills from them. Jane glanced interestedly through these then turned over the next cutting. It was from one of the more sensational dailies; the headline was stark and, coming after the previous material, shocking and lacking in taste. "World Famous Actor in Death Crash" read the large black letters. There was a photograph, thankfully blurred, of a Rolls Royce, that had been twisted and tortured into a wreck of torn metal. Jane's quick gaze scanned the print rapidly. Carstair's wife, Diane, had been driving; Carstairs sat beside her and his younger brother and his wife were in the back seat with Carstairs' son. Carstairs had survived as had his son, a baby of under two years, but the others were all killed instantly. It seemed that the child escaped without injury but Carstairs had been rushed to hospital and was, at the time of the article being printed, on the Dangerously Ill List. There were no details of his injuries but the articles that followed all drew the same picture and reached similar conclusions—they showed a man who had been very much in the public eye, withdrawing from it until he became near enough a recluse.

Jane looked at the photograph of Carstairs and his wife on their wedding day. Diane Carstairs looked very lovely, blonde and pale and coolly beautiful. It was a horrible story and she was aware of an ache of misery for a man who had lost so much.

"Finished?" Alistair's voice brought her abruptly back to the present and she nodded and closed the file.

"Whose fault was it? The accident I mean?"

"It was counted as an accident. The lorry driver insisted at the inquest that the Rolls went straight at him but there was a terrific thunderstorm at the time and the road was treacherous. Carstairs always maintained that he was unable to remember the few minutes leading up to the crash."

"Was he badly injured? Is that why he left the stage?" Jane supposed, with a self deprecating smile, that she had vague imaginings of a sort of "Phantom of the Opera" thing, a man so disfigured that he couldn't bear to show himself.

"I don't imagine so. I mean, he doesn't hide himself away down in the New Forest, which is where he lives. He visits his publisher in London and I've heard rumours of a lecture tour of the States sometime around Christmas. But he's very wary of publicity and once actually grabbed the camera from an enterprising young photographer and smashed it to smithereens. The thing is, Jane," Alistair went on, more earnest-ly now, coming to crouch at her feet and waving his hands expressively, "Carstairs is very newsworthy. A lot of our older readers will remember him, and they showed *Jane Eyre* on TV last weekend. And of course everyone has heard of his books or seen the films made of them. I want him, I want photographs and an article about his life since the accident, for *Looking Glass*."

Jane had guessed this much a few sentences back. It was typical of Alistair, she thought, that the ordinary human sympathy that would be aroused in most people on hearing the story of

Max Carstairs, would pass him by. He wouldn't care that the man might not care to be dragged back into the public eye. The story would sell his magazine and that was all that concerned Alistair.

"Why tell me this?" she inquired.

"Because I want you to get the info. and the photographs!" he promptly replied.

"Me?" Jane questioned, her voice rising to a squeak. "Why me? I'm not a reporter. I wouldn't know the first thing about how to go about it. And why should Max Carstairs talk to me as opposed to anyone else?"

"He won't, of course. There's no hope of gaining an interview. No, this must be handled with more subtlety, which is where you come in, Jane. Carstairs needs a secretary to help him with his latest book. His last girl left recently. He has put the appointing of the new girl in the hands of an agency and, as it happens, the owner of the agency owes me a favour and I can fix it so that you will be appointed. After all, you have the qualifications and should have no trouble handling the work. Carstairs would quickly get wise to a real reporter but you, Jane, are altogether too young and sweet and innocent looking to have anything to do with the tough world of journalism. There would be an interview of course, for the sake of appearances, but you'll definitely get the job."

Under different circumstances, Jane knew she would have jumped at the chance of being Max Carstairs' secretary, but the conditions by which she could ensure getting the job worried her. It sounded underhanded and distasteful, prying into the personal life of a man who had already been dealt a good many unhappy cards in his life.

"What do you say?" Alistair asked.

"I don't know," she murmured, shaking her head. "It's not very nice, prying into people's lives."

"All you have to do is report what you see—you won't have to pry. Naturally I'll let Carstairs see the article and approve it before we go to print. Think about the job itself, Jane." His voice dropped persuasively. "Imagine being instrumental in getting the latest Michael Collins book into print! Imagine talking to a man who has appeared on the most famous stages of the world, who has spoken the words of the greatest playwrights of all time!"

He was being clever all right, and she was sorely tempted. Her life was so *dull*—how could she refuse? Would she regret it all her life? She reopened the file and looked down at the top photograph, of Carstairs and his lovely wife on their wedding day. "No," she said firmly. "I can't do it. You must get someone else."

He tried for half an hour to make her change her mind but she was adamant. It was almost eight o'clock and she said firmly that she must go home. He drove her there, insisting that he would give her twenty-four hours to think about it.

"You do that," Jane said, smiling at his persistence. "But my answer will still be the same."

Jane lived with her mother in a three bedroomed bungalow on the outskirts of the small market town where she lived. Since James Murray died ten years earlier, his wife Isabel and his daughter had lived in a state of barely concealed animosity. Isabel—she had always encouraged Jane to call her that, presumably because "mother" made her seem too old—was forty-one and looked ten years younger. She owned a boutique in the town centre that she ran with success and flair and had never had much time for her daughter. Jane couldn't remember exactly when she discovered that she didn't like her mother, but she was young enough to be shocked by the fact. Only the discovery, as she grew into her teens, that Isabel did not like her either, reconciled her to a fact that had seemed unnatural and even wicked. Isabel made no attempt to hide the fact that Jane was a nuisance and a hindrance. Throughout her teenage years, Jane had drawn more and more into herself in order to conceal the hurt of being neither wanted nor loved, and through sheer self-preservation had learned not to show her feelings. She could no longer be hurt by Isabel; the bungalow was her home and sometimes Isabel was there and sometimes she was not. It really didn't matter, and perversity as much as anything else had stopped her looking round for somewhere else to live. She didn't see why she should be forced out of her home so that Isabel could entertain her many men friends without the embarrassment of having to introduce a twenty-three year old daughter. Some of the friends were scarcely older than Jane.

When she got indoors, Jane hung her raincoat in the hall and went into the lounge where she was dismayed to discover Malcolm Harris, Isabel's latest and most ardent admirer. In his early thirties, Harris was dark haired, almost excessively good looking, and Jane loathed him. When she first met him, he had treated Jane with amused contempt and hadn't been above ridiculing her, her clothes, her looks, her attitude to life. Then, subtly and far more alarmingly, his attitude had changed. One day, when the two of them were alone in the bungalow, he followed her into her bedroom, grabbing her and kissing her, and only her quick reactions, in kicking his shins and running to lock herself in the bathroom until Isabel came in, had averted a very unpleasant scene. Since then he had never lost an opportunity of touching her, whenever and wherever he could, as though her resistance to his charms enflamed him more. Jane never mentioned this behaviour to Isabel. It was unlikely that Isabel would believe in her purely passive role and was sure to think she had encouraged Harris. It would be unthinkable that any man admiring the lovely Isabel could ever want her plain and dull daughter.

Jane had always managed since to avoid being alone with Harris. Now she headed for her bedroom which had a good, strong lock but she was beaten to it by Harris who barred her way into the hall.

"Don't go, Jane darling. We never get the chance to be alone, do we? And you know I'm crazy about you." He reached for her but she jerked away.

"Leave me alone! You know what happened last time."

"Oh, that! Playing hard to get, weren't you? You must know how that gets a man going. Come on now, be nice."

"I wouldn't be nice to you if you were the last man on earth!" she whispered, her voice violent with disgust. "Can't you take a hint? I hate you!"

His good looking face became ugly with anger as he grabbed her shoulders. "Listen, sweetie, you aren't so brilliant that you can afford to talk to anyone like that. I must have been out of my mind even to look twice at you. A man would need to be half blind to look at a plain creature like you!"

Although she hated him, the words could not fail to hurt. Jane flinched and twisted away from him, white and trembling; she came up hard against the settee and sat down with a bump. Harris's mouth twisted into a laugh that also sneered and he was about to follow her down when they heard the front door open. When Isabel came in, very expensive looking in a knee length silver fox coat, Jane was sitting on the settee and Harris was standing some way from her in the process of lighting a cigarette. He smiled broadly at Isabel, said, "Darling!" and went over to kiss her passionately, while Jane got unsteadily to her feet, feeling sick, and headed for her room.

"Wait a minute, Jane," Isabel called. She was smiling up at Harris, holding his arm. "Have you told her the good news, darling?"

"I thought I'd wait till you came in." He looked directly at Jane. "You must congratulate us, Jane. Isabel has agreed to be my wife."

During the ensuing moments, while Jane fought the desire to either vomit there and then or burst into hysterical laughter, nothing was said, then she took a deep breath and managed to say, "That's very nice. Congratulations, Isabel, Malcolm."

Isabel was in a very genial, expansive mood. She flung her arms round her daughter, who was permitted to peck her powdered cheek, getting a strong whiff of her French perfume as she did so. Then she was forced to stand still while Harris kissed her lingeringly on the mouth. Isabel seemed to find this action quite acceptable and laughed, cooing, "Just think, darlings, in a little while, Malcolm will be Jane's step father!"

At this point, Jane thought rather sourly, an hour later, we should all have fallen about laughing. In fact the remark had been greeted stonily by both Malcolm and herself. She wasn't a bit bothered about Isabel getting married again, and if she wanted to land herself with a smarmy little squirt like Malcolm Harris, she was welcome. One thing was certain, though. She, Jane, couldn't go on living in the bungalow with them. If Isabel had been marrying any other man she would have been reluctant, but with Harris it was unthinkable. Now she would have to get out—and soon.

A quick glance through the evening paper told her that small flats and bed sitters were few and far between. It seemed as though she was being pushed relentlessly towards accepting Alistair's proposition. Wasn't it, after all, just what she wanted? An exciting new job which entailed living in? Before she had time to change her mind, before her conscience could prod her into a quick reversal, she rang the number Alistair had given her.

"I'm not going to pry into Max Carstairs' private life," she still emphatically insisted. "And you must promise me you'll print nothing without his permission."

"Of course I promise," he agreed readily. "Leave everything to me, Jane dear. I'll soon fix it up."

The interview was in London, at the Marston Employment Agency and was, as Alistair had predicted, a mere formality. There were three other applicants, all older women convinced they would get the job and that Jane stood no chance. "I believe Mr. Collins actually stipulated an older woman," one of them said, looking meaningfully at Jane. She felt an uneasy twinge of guilt; it seemed underhanded and she would much rather have got the job on merit. It wasn't as though her qualifications were not good, after all. But then she remembered Malcolm Harris and her guilt was hastily suppressed.

Isabel was in the midst of preparations for her wedding and far too busy to take much notice when Jane mentioned the interview. But now she went home and announced that in a fortnight's time she would be off to Hampshire. Isabel stared at her aghast, and then calmed down, saying with the sort of voice one would use to humour a child, "Don't be ridiculous, Jane. Of course you aren't going anywhere."

"I am!" Jane insisted emphatically. "The Saturday after next in fact."

"My dear Jane, don't you realise I shall need you here at the time of the wedding?" Isabel continued to speak in the same humouring tones as she unpacked the purchases she had bought that day, lifting from boxes filled with tissue paper gossamer-light underwear, expensive crocodile skin shoes and handbags, a pure silk evening gown. Jane, who never spent in a year a quarter the amount this lot must have cost, looked on in silence as her mother went on, "There will be people staying here overnight, who will need looking after; there are the presents to see to—oh, a million other things I shall need you for. Now, be a good girl and help me pack these things away. I rather think I shall need a new set of luggage. I saw some beautiful pig skin cases in town today."

Jane bit back the hasty, furious comments that rose to her lips and strengthened her will against being bull dozed in this way. "You don't really need me, Isabel," she said frankly and reasonably. "You'll get someone else to help you, you know you will. This is a marvellous opportunity for me to do something exciting with my life and I can't turn it down. Let me tell you about it."

But Isabel, seeming to accept, from the calm, even tones that Jane used, that she meant what she said, refused to listen. Holding in her hands a beautiful nightdress of heavy, pale-green satin trimmed with real lace, she regarded Jane with cold dislike and Jane knew without doubt that the veneer between them, that said they should at least pretend to be fond of each other for convention's sake, was gone forever. She was struck chill by it, though not saddened. "I might have known you would do something like this!" Isabel cried, her blue eyes snapping fire. "Of all the selfish, ungrateful creatures I've ever known, you take the cake! You are just doing this to make things awkward for me!"

Any doubts Jane may have had fled. From now on, she knew, she was on her own. There would be no coming back here if the job with Max Carstairs didn't work out.

"I'm going," she said, quietly and firmly, and turned away.

Two

Jane saw Alistair several times during the following fortnight, for he had decided to stay in town, he said for a holiday, but Jane suspected it was to make sure she didn't change her mind. They dined in the best restaurants, went for drives in the country, he took her to the theatre. Alistair was very charming and Jane wondered more than once why she hadn't fallen in love with him all over again. But always, at the back of her mind, was the feeling that he was putting it on. He wasn't really interested in her; he knew she had reservations about the job she was going to undertake and was trying to reconcile her to it by proving to her what a fundamentally decent chap he was. But Jane wasn't fooled. She *did* have reservations and if it hadn't been for the really dreadful atmosphere at home since the scene with Isabel, she might still have backed out. She finally decided that if it really did prove too difficult to probe into Max Carstairs' private life, she could always leave. She wasn't bound by any contract but was using Alistair in order to escape Isabel and Malcolm. Just as Alistair was using her. Surely the only reason he had recruited her was because she wasn't connected with *Looking*

Glass and if things did back fire, Carstairs couldn't pin anything on the magazine. Jane suggested this quite bluntly to Alistair on the day he drove her up to London where she was to catch the Southampton train from Waterloo station.

"Nonsense, my dear. You've grown very cynical," he denied, laughing a little uncertainly. "As though such a thought would cross my mind."

"All right," Jane agreed. "Perhaps I'm wrong. But I reserve the right to get out if things don't go as planned. I don't intend bringing any more unhappiness to Max Carstairs."

"Don't you worry, Jane. Just relax and let things take their course. And don't forget, give yourself a few weeks to settle in before you start the real job. The last thing we want is for Carstairs to kick you out for being nosey."

They were sitting in the self-service café on the station. There was a quarter of an hour to go before the train was due to leave, and Alistair went to fetch two more cups of coffee. When he returned, he drew heavily on his cigarette and seemed to be debating something to himself, finally saying, "I suppose I'd better warn you. Carstairs is supposed to be rather difficult to get on with. His last secretary left after a bit of a blow up. Apparently her opinion is that Carstairs is arrogant, bad-tempered and completely insensitive to anyone's feelings."

Jane's eyes widened and she sat up straighter. "Now he tells me! Really, Alistair, the man sounds an absolute monster. Can I change my mind?"

He knew she was joking; she had no choice but to go on. If she turned her back on Max Carstairs she would have no home to go to and no job. As they walked across to the train, Alistair put one arm lightly round her shoulders. "The way to get on with him is to work hard and not answer back. Put up with his temper." He smiled winningly at her. "You'll be all right, Jane. You seem to get on well enough with most people. Just melt into the background and I daresay Carstairs won't notice you."

"I'll do my best," Jane muttered with trepidation. He kissed her and watched as she carried her case through the ticket barrier to the train. She looked such a forlorn, slender young figure that even Alistair had his doubts about her ability to carry out his instructions.

The train was a slow one, stopping at every station between Waterloo and Southampton, so Jane expected a long journey. She had brought with her the latest Michael Collins thriller, reckoning she ought to get up to date with the work of her new employer. During the greatest part of the journey she had the carriage to herself and apart from reading the first two chapters of *Ice Fall*, she looked dreamily out of the window, watching the scenery as it evolved through its various stages from city to calm, ordered middle-class suburbia, to red and yellow autumn countryside. It began to rain before the train had left London behind and Jane wondered what it would be like to live in the country, in the very centre of the New Forest. Would it seem lonely, or unbearably quiet? She was a city girl and knew very little about rural life but she had never—at least since Alistair walked out of her life—been one for getting about much. Her chief delight was to curl up in front of the fire with a good book, and about the only time she bothered to venture out was when she went to the theatre. And who could possibly regret the loss of this particular form of entertainment when they would be breathing the same air as Max Carstairs himself? A little smile touched Jane's calm mouth. Alistair's parting words about Carstairs hadn't really worried her. To meet the actor had been the height of her ambition for years; it was the equivalent of a ballet lover suddenly coming face to face with Nureyev, or an opera fan with Callas! How could she fail to be filled with expectancy and delight?

The employment agency had furnished her details about her journey. She would be met at the station where she was to alight from the train, for there was no public transport within a mile of Mill House, which was the name of Carstairs' residence. When the train arrived it was six o'clock, getting dark and still raining heavily. Jane shivered in her thin coat and headed for the station entrance. She felt cold and hungry; it was dark and wet and the street outside the station was deserted. After waiting ten minutes she returned to the ticket collector who seemed also to be the porter and station master. He was sitting in a warm office cradling a cup of tea and reading the Daily Mirror.

"Can you tell me how far it is to Mill House? I was supposed to have been met but there's no one about."

"Ah, that would be Mr. Philip," he told her, looking at her without curiosity. "I saw him here earlier. Reckon he went over to the Black Swan across the way. You'll see his car in the car park I daresay. A mean looking red thing it is. You'd best go and fetch him out else he'll be there till closing time."

"Thank you," Jane said shortly. She didn't know who "Mr. Philip" was but she felt fit to brain him, certainly too angry to feel in any way embarrassed about marching into the Black

Swan and demanding of the landlord which of his customers was "Mr. Philip."

"He's in the public, miss. I'll call him. Who shall I say wants him?" He repeated her name and went off, leaving Jane to sit in one of the comfortable armchairs by the fire that burned brightly in the otherwise empty lounge bar. A moment later the door opened and a tall young man in a brown suède jacket came in. He stood in the doorway, surveying her with brown eyes that showed a gleam of interest, and asked, "Are you Jane Murray?"

"I am." Jane stood up, stretching her five feet four inches to their limit. "I believe you were supposed to meet me."

"Yes I was. Sorry I wasn't there, but let's face it, British Rail is seldom on time." He smiled so charmingly and apologetically that Jane forgave him. She suspected he was one of those thankfully rare men that can all too easily get their own way with a bit of flattery and a sweet, little-boy smile. He bought her a whisky and introduced himself as Philip Marks.

"I'm Max's brother-in-law," he explained. "You do know that Michael Collins is really Max Carstairs?"

Jane nodded. "They . . . ah, told me at the agency," she explained, hoping she wasn't blushing at the lie. This was not going to be quite as easy as she had imagined.

"You're much younger than we expected you to be," Philip told her. "Max has always chosen his own secretaries before, and real old dragons they are too! This is the first time he's left the appointment in the hands of an agency. I'm sure he mentioned that he stipulated an older woman." He laughed suddenly. "The last one was like an all-in wrestler. She tried to run the whole household and even Max couldn't get the better of her until they had a stand up row and she left in a huff. The one before that fell in love with him and tried to reform him. Whatever *you* do, Jane Murray, don't look disapprovingly upon him."

"Am I likely to?" Jane asked lightly.

"I don't know. He's a little hard to take sometimes. He's got a foul temper when anything gets him going."

Suddenly Jane was angry with this self-satisfied young man. What could he know about losing a wife, a brother and a sister-in-law all in one fell swoop? Wasn't that enough to alter any man, to change him beyond recognition? Yet here he was, discussing Max Carstairs with her, a complete stranger, and it seemed almost as though he enjoyed watching his brother-in-law behaving badly. She glanced at her watch.

"I think we should go. Mr. Carstairs will be expecting me."

"He isn't home at the moment. He's in London on his yearly visit to his publisher. Still, we may as well go. I suppose I oughtn't to have another drink." As they walked to his car, a red M.G. two-seater, he at last seemed to sense Jane's disapproval for he turned to her, smiling charmingly. "Don't be mad at me for talking to you about Max. I was just trying to put you on your guard. You do look very young and innocent and he can be an awkward character."

"I am quite capable of taking care of myself, thank you, Mr. Marks," Jane replied, a trifle primly because she felt so cross. "And I think perhaps I should be allowed to form my own opinions."

He was undaunted, saying, as he opened the

car door for her, "Call me Philip, please. No doubt we'll be seeing quite a lot of each other while you're at Mill House." So saying, he started up the powerful little car with a roar and they shot off into the wet evening. In no time at all they had bumped over a cattle grid that stretched across the road, and Philip said they were now in the New Forest proper. "The grids are to keep the animals in the vicinity of the forest, off the main roads and out of the towns. It's too dark to see much now but when the weather's fine the forest is well worth a visit."

"Do you live at Mill House?" Jane asked and he shook his head.

"I've got a pad in London but I come down here quite often. I work for Max too, a sort of unofficial agent—a go-between between Max and his publisher. He goes to London sometimes but only if he can't avoid it. He prefers to pay someone else to handle that side of his work. And when I'm in town I occasionally do the odd bit of research for him."

Jane glanced at his profile. "You say Mr. Carstairs is bad tempered, yet you work for him."

"I've known Max for years and I'm used to him. Besides, I'm not a woman." On this cryptic note, the conversation was broken off abruptly as he turned the car sharply to the left, saying, "Here we are, Mill House. And don't ask me why the name because there isn't a mill in miles." The car rattled over another cattle grid, this one designed to keep the forest ponies out, and ran up a long, curved drive to the house.

It was a huge, rambling place though not, Jane guessed, all that old, with red tiled roof and walls of flint. It was too wet for Jane to more than glimpse the silhouette of the house against the stormy sky, a silhouette of many tall chimneys and slanting roofs, and, amazingly, a round turretlike structure straight from a fairy story. Or a horror film, Jane thought with brief humour, and she saw it as a sort of Dracula's castle, with Max Carstairs, fearfully scarred and twisted by the accident, prowling about the long dark corridors.

"It looks as though a mad man built it," Philip said, pulling up the collar of his jacket and making a dash for the porch. "Imagine building a sort of Gothic castle in the middle of Hampshire." He shook rain off his thick brown hair and smiled. "Actually it was once a very select public school for boys. Max himself was educated here, which is why he bought it when the school closed down." He pulled the huge bell pull and in a moment the door was opened by a trim girl who wore a navy dress and frilly white apron. Philip led Jane inside, handing his jacket to the girl.

"Hello, Beth. This is Miss Murray. Jane, this is Beth. She looks after Simon, Max's son, when he is here."

Jane returned the girl's smile and tried not to gape round at her surroundings with open-mouthed amazement. But she couldn't quite ignore them. She felt as though she had stepped back into the Middle Ages. The hall was vast, so vast that its far reaches were lost in gloom. The floor was a giant chess board of black and white tiles that stretched away in all directions. Several doors opened off the hall but the main feature was an enormous staircase of polished oak that gleamed warmly in the electric light, and, at its foot, a real, genuine suit of armour. Jane blinked hard and glanced at Philip, who was grinning.

"It's not authentic, of course, but quite spectacular for all that. Don't worry, the rest of the house has been modernised, but Max couldn't bring himself to do anything with the hall."

"I'm glad. It's wonderful," Jane enthused. "Once you've got over the shock."

While they were talking, someone else appeared from the far end of the hall, a comfortable looking woman who was introduced to Jane as Mrs. Hoskyns, the housekeeper. She shook Jane's hand firmly and led her upstairs to her room. At the top the staircase split into two, forming a gallery that led all the way round the hall and from which all the bedrooms led. Jane's room was to the left; to her relief it couldn't have been more cheerful or modern, with a neat divan bed covered in a white silk quilt, and warmed by a fire in the grate. It was a pretty room and Jane smiled at the bowl of chrysanthemums on the white dressing table.

"I thought they would cheer up the place, my dear," the housekeeper smiled as Jane thanked her. "Now, I'll leave you to unpack and have a rest. Dinner will be ready in an hour so if you will just ring the bell when you are ready, I'll send one of the maids up to show you the way, otherwise you might get lost. The bathroom is just through that door."

"Thank you," Jane murmured. The housekeeper gave her a friendly though curious look and then smiled. "It will seem strange at first, no doubt, for Mill House *is* rather overwhelming, but you will soon settle in. Despite it's appearance, the house is really quite friendly and Mr. Carstairs is a wonderful man to work for. Why, I've been with the family since I was a girl so I should know."

When she had gone, Jane crouched by the fire

warming her hands and thinking, so he's a wonderful man to work for, is he? This was a different picture from the one painted by Philip. Different though not necessarily contradictory. She supposed Max Carstairs was capable of being pleasant to his staff if only to keep them from walking out on him.

As there would be only herself and Philip for dinner, Jane changed into a neat skirt and blouse, reasoning that she would not be expected to dress more formally. She had no idea what the arrangements for her meals would be when her employer was at home. It was possible that she would be expected to eat with the other members of staff. She combed out her fair hair and pinned it back into its neat chignon before ringing the bell and following the maid, this time another girl who introduced herself as Sally, to the dining room.

During dinner, a well-cooked meal served by Beth, Philip filled Jane in on details of the household. Apart from Mrs. Hoskyns who also did the cooking, and the two maids, there was an odd-job man and a woman who came in from the village four times a week to help with the general housework. When Jane mentioned that this seemed a lot of people to look after one man, Philip explained. "Max has a lot of visitors and he merely kept on the staff after Diane's death. I'm down quite often and of course there's Simon, Max's six-year-old son. And Margot is down here more often than in her own home." Jane merely looked an enquiry and he explained. "Margot Copeland. She was a close friend of Max's before Diane came on the scene, and has just lately taken to following Max around."

It was clear that Philip didn't approve of Margot

Copeland but Jane wisely didn't pursue the subject. Whatever the relationship between her employer and Margot, it had nothing whatsoever to do with her. She took her thoughts away from Philip's rather strident "county" voice and looked at her surroundings. The room they sat in was large but of pleasant proportions, with long mullioned windows hung with midnight-blue velvet drapes; Jane particularly admired the wood panelling that glowed warmly in the light from the chandelier that hung from the centre of the ceiling. The polished mahogany table was circular, an unusual innovation that she guessed led to greater intimacy during a dinner party, and the chair seats were tapestry covered. With a log fire blazing in the huge stone fireplace, it was a warm, friendly room.

She returned to Philip's voice, hearing him speak his brother-in-law's name again. "Margot seems to be about the only woman to bring out any human feelings in him. I know you don't approve of me warning you about Max, but a warning is in order. He's hard and cold and, apart from his feelings for Simon, which are genuine enough, he has completely cut himself off from ordinary warm, human emotions. In some ways he's the most cold-blooded bastard in the world."

"Perhaps he has a reason," Jane suggested quietly.

"The accident, you mean? Oh, sure, but that was four years ago and Max was more upset about Brian, his brother, and his wife being killed than about Diane. It wasn't as though Max and Diane were even living together then. They loathed each other." He looked into Jane's shocked face and shrugged. "She was my sister but I can't say I blamed Max. Diane never made any secret of the fact that she married Max because he was wealthy and famous. Anyway, that's beside the point. Max will expect you to work as hard as he does himself. Don't go seeing him as a romantic character, a bitter, heart-broken man just waiting for the right woman to come along and sort him out. He's more likely to do the heartbreaking. Apart from Margot, he doesn't have a lot of respect for women, so make sure you keep your relationship with him on a business footing."

"I'm not likely to do anything else," Jane replied, rather stiffly.

"No. You look too sensible to go throwing yourself at him like some of these stupid women do. Besides, I shouldn't think he'd look twice at you." Something flickered over Jane's face as he said these words. Of course, he could not know about Malcolm Harris' similar statement, but he was immediately apologetic. "Don't take that the wrong way. I don't mean because you're not worth looking at. It's just that when Max bothers to look at a woman, he goes for the sophisticated types, the sort that know the name of the game."

Having extricated himself from a difficult position, with the adroitness of a man used to a full social life and with the confidence this life produced, he turned the subject to less personal topics and the rest of the meal progressed quite happily.

Sunday was spent by Jane exploring Mill House and its immediate grounds. Philip joined her for breakfast, announcing his intention of spending the day with some friends in Southampton. He invited Jane to join him but she declined. She felt she needed the day to settle into

Mill House, familiarising herself with her new surroundings before Max Carstairs returned. After Philip had left, she found her way to the library where Carstairs did most of his work. It was a long, rectangular room with a domed ceiling fantastically painted with scenes from Greek Mythology. The two long walls were covered with books, a vast, indigestible assortment, haphazardly placed as though they had never been catalogued or even read. At the far end of the room, opposite the door, was a large window of stained glass through which the sunlight poured, sending patterns of reds, greens, blues and yellows over the dark brown carpet. Involuntarily, Jane smiled. It was a lovely room in which to work, a lovely, peaceful room that seemed to welcome her as though she had spoken. Strange that it was here that Max Carstairs' exciting, tense and often violent stories evolved.

Jane walked round the room, her feet making no noise on the deep-pile Wilton carpet. Near the window was a large mahogany desk with a green leather writing surface and, beside it, a smaller one, more modern and equipped with an electric typewriter. Jane sat at this desk, opening the drawers and discovering the whereabouts of all the tools of her trade: bank and bond paper, carbons, spare typewriter ribbons, note pads and pencils. She familiarised herself with the positioning of everything and even had a quick practice on the typewriter. Max Carstairs wanted efficiency, did he? Well, she would be so efficient he would have no cause for complaint.

Yesterday's rains had turned to warm autumn sunshine and after lunch Jane walked round the gardens. There were some ten acres of grounds surrounding the house and she enjoyed a pleasant afternoon just rambling about. She discovered a tumbledown, pagoda-style summer house now inhabited only by spiders and a family of field mice, a rose garden, much overgrown and uncared for, and a very neat vegetable garden.

"The gardens are very neglected," Mrs. Hoskyns told Jane as she served her dinner. "The gardens were beautiful when Mrs. Carstairs was alive, and she always saw to that side of things. There was a gardener then, but he got too old and Mr. Carstairs never bothered to employ another. It's a shame; the roses in the rose garden used to look a real treat. I do the vegetable garden myself," she explained. "With Johns, the odd-jobber doing the heavy work. If there's one thing I can't abide, it's shop bought vegetables when I can grow my own."

After dinner Jane returned to the library, browsing for a while among the books, but eventually drawn to the windows that overlooked the lawns. There was a three-quarter moon that lit everything outside—the row of beech trees that bordered the drive, the long flight of steps leading from the front porch of the house down to the ground level—with a ghostly, grey light. Jane wondered what the house would look like in the moonlight and suspected it would be more like Dracula's castle than ever. On impulse she pushed open the French windows and stepped on to the flagged patio outside. It was cold but she wore a dress of pale blue wool with a close fitting bodice, a high neck and long fitted sleeves; a warm, snug dress with a full skirt that floated round her legs as she ran swiftly across the lawn. The long, straggly grass swished softly against her ankles as she moved. For someone who had lived all her life in the town, the fresh air, the unutterable stillness, were like a heady wine. An owl hooted eerily in the trees and somewhere far away a dog howled. Jane shivered with excitement that was also fear and turned to look at the house. Unexpectedly, bathed in moonlight, it was beautiful. She was amazed at how black the shadows were, shadows of strange-shaped roofs and chimneys, turrets and garrets. Here and there the moonlight caught on a window and flashed back a silver-white reflection. Jane stood in the middle of the lawn, her head thrown back, as she gazed at the house, her arms folded across her chest, hugging her happiness to herself.

Suddenly she was so happy, so free, that it couldn't be contained. The lawn stretched before her like a dance floor and, as though it were just that, she began to waltz, holding an imaginary partner and humming "The Blue Danube." Her skirt whirled round her as did her long fine silvery blonde hair, loosed from its usual restraining chignon.

It was only after she had happily waltzed twice round the lawn that Jane realised, with a shock of fear that caused her heart to leap and even, for a moment, made the hair prickle on her scalp, that she was being watched.

The man stood on the patio by the library, silhouetted darkly against the light from the house. He appeared to be dressed completely in black and Jane saw only his shape, tall and broad-shouldered, a very big, relaxed body, and the red glowing tip of his cigarette. The moonlight glinted on his hair. She stood quite still, biting her lip uncertainly, while her heart continued to lurch sickeningly against her ribs.

"Very nice," the man remarked in a lazy, drawling voice. "Should I request an encore?"

Jane's eyes closed in brief despair as she recognised the voice; it was one of the most well-known voices in England, or had been until a few years ago. She had first heard it speaking the inspired and stirring words of Shakespeare's Henry V when she was ten years old, and knew she would never forget it. She took a deep breath but even this, and slowly counting to ten, did not still her frightened heart or give her back her voice.

He dropped the cigarette and ground it beneath one foot. "Don't you know you're trespassing?" he inquired, quite pleasantly. Jane managed to shake her head and licked dry lips as she swallowed convulsively. "Not that I object to you using my lawn as a dance floor, but trespassers, you know, are generally punished in some way, or a forfeit is required."

At that moment the moon floated behind a cloud and the world was pitched into darkness, save for the pale glow that fell on him from the library window. Jane took an uncertain step backwards, sure that now was the time to make her escape. She couldn't see his face at all well and it was possible that he couldn't see hers either. Perhaps he would not recognise her again. It was a vain hope but the only one she had. She took another step, half turning and poised for flight, but before she could make her retreat he had moved, so swiftly that suddenly he was beside her, his hands gripping her shoulders. She tried to pull away, an involuntary cry of protest on her lips, but her indignant objection was cut off short as his mouth swooped down and fastened on hers. After a moment of paralysing panic, she struggled with all her strength,

having always despised those silly girls in novels
who allow men to kiss them against their will
with scarcely a struggle. Surely, she had always
reasoned, there was something that could be
done! Even if it was a violent action such as a
sharp kick on the shins, an action that proved to
be most effective when used on Malcolm Harris.
Here, however, was a far stronger and more-to-be-
reckoned-with antagonist; he was a different
proposition altogether for she found to her cha-
grin that it is difficult to do anything very much
when you are pulled hard against a lean, strongly-
muscled body that is straining fiercely against
you, when your breath is cut off very nearly
completely by a passionate, demanding mouth. It
was only when he himself relaxed his grip on her,
that Jane managed to pull her mouth away and
gasp, "Oh, let me go! How dare you!" in such an
affronted voice that he actually laughed. He took
his arms from round her, retaining the grip on
her wrists as she attempted to escape.

"Don't run away. I won't kiss you again. Not
now anyway. That's not to say I wouldn't like to
but I shall only exact one forfeit. Tell me who you
are." His voice was beautiful, well-modulated and
perfectly pitched, the trained voice of an actor,
that could do anything its owner asked of it. It
could shake with emotion, bellow with rage, it
could freeze or it could caress. Jane said nothing;
she was too shaken to speak a word and after a
moment she felt the hold of her wrists relax.

"A mystery, eh? I like mysteries, especially a
mysterious young woman with hair like silver
who comes from nowhere and dances on my lawn
like a wood nymph. I am very much afraid, wood
nymph, that if you do not tell me who you are, I

shall have to exact another forfeit." His voice was now heavy with seduction, flowing over Jane like a silken caress and she knew only too well what he meant. For a moment, as he came closer and she felt his warm breath upon her lips, she remained there, staring at him as his head, the face still shrouded in darkness, came towards her, and briefly she felt the temptation of his voice and touch, and weakened under them, wanting to stay there, returning his kisses. But then he laughed softly and the little sound reasserted her common sense and it was the sensible, practical Jane, who most emphatically did not allow herself to be kissed by strange men, who jerked her hands away from his grip and ran away, round the side of the house, her feet making no sound on the grass. There was a door at the side that she had discovered during her afternoon's explorations, that was luckily still unlocked, and through here she slipped, running softly up to her bedroom. She was trembling and stricken with the desire to burst into tears, which was, she told herself sternly, very stupid. She should be feeling furious, not upset; who did the man think he was anyway, going round kissing people in that insufferable, arrogant way as though every female was bound to enjoy his caresses?

Later Jane analysed her feelings more carefully and came to the conclusion that she was miserable because she knew that now she could not possibly stay on at Mill House. Apart from the fact that she was obviously unable to cope with Max Carstairs, she was also terrified of meeting him again and having to admit that the silly girl who was dancing on his lawn was also his "efficient" secretary! The only thing to do, she decided in a flash of uncharacteristic panic, was to pack her suitcases and get out. It was no good going there and then, of course. It was past ten o'clock and she had no idea where to go. She would leave early, at first light, before anyone else was up; there was bound to be a telephone kiosk out on the main road somewhere, where she could ring for a taxi to take her to the station. By the time the household was up and about, she would be gone. Alistair and his magazine were forgotten as she set her alarm clock for five and crawled into bed to try to get some sleep.

The massive front door was very securely locked, not just with a modern Yale lock but with three bolts and a chain. Jane put her suitcase down and began to tackle the bolts; they were well-oiled and slid back easily and with no noise, but she had trouble with the chain and cursed softly as she broke a finger nail on it. It was almost light outside but no daylight had yet permeated the huge gloomy hall of Mill House, so that Jane could not see very well. She had at last managed to loose the chain when a voice said, "Stay where you are!"

Jane jumped in fright at the peremptory sound and turned towards the voice. She realised, with sickening fear, that the speaker was at the top of the staircase which was swathed in gloom, and that she knew the voice. No one else could have produced such strident, ringing tones without even shouting. In a moment his figure appeared out of the darkness. He was still wearing dark clothing; black corded pants encased long slim legs and a black polo neck sweater completed the outfit. Finally his head came into view, though it was still so dark, where he stood beside the suit of armour at the foot of the stairs, that Jane couldn't make out his features, just the pale blur of his face topped by thick black hair.

"Well, well," he said softly, his voice echoing a little in the huge hall. "If it isn't the wood nymph. Am I to continue running into you in strange places? What are you doing creeping about my house at this time of the morning?"

"I was leaving," Jane gulped. "You oughtn't to be up yet!"

Her tone was accusatory and a little childish, so that not surprisingly, he laughed. "I never went to bed," he said coolly. "Stay there!"

He moved over to the wall near her and reached out one hand, clicking on a hidden switch so that the hall was flooded with light from the huge central chandelier, a light so momentarily blinding that Jane blinked and rubbed her eyes. When her vision was right again she looked up into Max Carstairs' face. Her gasp was purely voluntary, neither of dismay nor disgust, though she supposed horror had a part in it. Her reaction, she later decided, was the same as it would have been had she seen the Mona Lisa, or any other perfect work of art, slashed with a razor. That was all the horror was, that anything as beautiful as Max Carstairs' face could be so disfigured. The scar began about an inch from his left eye and ran down his cheek to his jaw line. It wasn't a neat scar either, as from a surgeon's knife, but was white and puckered and sometimes a little pulse throbbed in it. For the life of her, Jane couldn't pretend it wasn't there. Her eyes lingered on it while pity for him flooded in a warm tide over her.

She didn't pity him for being scarred, but for the memories it must conjure up every time he looked in a mirror. She forgot completely that last night this man had treated her so badly.

His mouth twisted at her expression and he said, a little bitterly, "I suppose I should have left the light off. What's the matter, wood nymph? Does the sight of me fascinate you that much? The fascination of the perfect for the imperfect?"

The idea of him calling her perfect was so ludicrous that Jane felt her lips twitch into a smile that brought a puzzled frown to his brow. She found it hard to believe he didn't realise that, scar or no scar, he was the most devastatingly attractive man she had ever met in her life, or was likely to meet.

"You find me amusing?" he demanded coldly, raising one eyebrow in an imperious gesture she remembered from *Antony and Cleopatra*.

She wondered if actors ever stopped acting. Where did they draw the line between real behaviour and a sort of naturally inbred sense of drama? Jane remembered her father once saying that just because actors tended to over-emphasize emotion, it didn't necessarily mean they weren't being sincere.

"No," she replied calmly. "I don't find you amusing, Mr. Carstairs. Just a little . . . melo-dramatic." She held her breath as she spoke, but she was no longer afraid of him. For a moment she had glimpsed something behind the confident mask of his face—something so elusive she could scarcely put a name to it—bitterness certainly but also loneliness and even . . . though it seemed ridiculous to say it, vulnerability. As though he could be hurt quite easily if the wrong nerve was touched. Suddenly Jane knew she wanted to stay here, that it would be unbearable to go away and never see him again.

"Melodramatic!" he repeated in astonishment. "My God, you little . . ." He stopped speaking, holding down his anger without difficulty, as though it had been assumed for appearances' sake rather than actually felt. "At least now, having delivered that *coup de grâce* you might tell me who you are."

"I'm Jane Murray."

"And who is Jane Murray? Am I supposed to know you?"

"I—I'm your secretary," she ventured uncertainly.

"My what?" he thundered, so that for the second time that morning Jane nearly jumped out of her skin. "My secretary? Like hell you are!"

"I am . . . really. The Marston Employment Agency hired me."

"I stipulated a woman of at least forty. Not a schoolgirl!"

"I'm not a schoolgirl!" Jane cried indignantly. "I'm twenty-three years old."

"Twenty-three? Huh!" he snorted, and pointed to the middle of the hall. "Stand there!"

She meekly obeyed, walking across the black and white chequered floor, a neat, slender figure in her navy blue slacks and woollen jacket, her hair pinned up smoothly into its customary chignon, and waited, hands clasped nervously in front of her, head lowered. She had thought at one point that she was handling the situation quite well but now was beginning to feel that she was being manipulated by this dazzlingly attractive, unpredictable man. He walked round her twice, an action guaranteed to unnerve anyone, eyeing her up and down in an impersonal assessment, rather as a man might view a race horse. Finally he halted in front of her, hands dug deep into trouser pockets, waiting until she was forced to raise her eyes to his, and saying, bluntly, "Why didn't you tell me last night who you were?"

Jane had hoped he wouldn't refer to that particular incident and now blushed unhappily at the recollection, protesting hotly, "You hardly gave me a chance to say anything! Anyway, would it have made any difference?"

"As it happens, yes, it would have. Despite what you may have heard to the contrary, I do not go round kissing my employees. Such a relationship is not conducive to work."

"I don't suppose it is," Jane agreed in a weak voice, her blush receding fast in the fact of his impersonal attitude. She now felt hopelessly out of her depths.

"Besides which, I don't go in for cradle snatching," he added shortly, turning abruptly on his heels and stalking away from her, his footsteps echoing hollowly on the tiled floor. When he was lost in the darkness of the far end of the hall, his footsteps halted. "Come on, girl!" he snapped.

"Where to?" Jane asked, running after him.

"You say you're my secretary. Before I confirm that, I want to see if you're capable of such a job."

Over the next hour Jane wondered more than once if she had ventured into a nightmare or a mad house. It was not yet dawn yet here she was expected to be wide awake and at her most efficient. He led her to the library, indicated the desk which she had previously looked through and, before she had time to do more than grab notebook and pencil, began dictating in a rapid, staccato voice. Jane had no time to think or get more than the vaguest notion of what she was scribbling. Her pencil flashed across page after page and by the time he stopped talking, as abruptly as he had begun, she was sweating and wondering in a panic if he always worked this way. If so, it explained how he managed to produce two full-length novels a year and why he had such a rapid turnover of secretaries. Had any of them died of exhaustion? she wondered. She closed her eyes and pulled her scattered wits about her. "Is that all?"

"For the moment. Did you get it all down?"

Jane nodded and was permitted the luxury of feeling pleased with herself for about ten seconds, that is, before he said, "Right, type it out. I want two carbon copies within the hour. Everything you need is in the desk." He turned to walk out.

"Mr. Carstairs!" Jane shouted, her voice coming out like a squeak of terror. He turned and looked impatiently at her. "It's not yet six o'clock," she said, trying not to sound whining, wishing she had not spoken at all. But suddenly she felt exhausted and even hungry. Max Carstairs, looking almost devilish, dressed all in black as he was, and with that dreadful scar marring his beautiful face, smiled grimly and said, "So? If you want to work for me, girl, you must get used to these hours. Why do you think I pay such high wages? Not for some mealy-mouthed creature that can only work from nine to five. If I want you to work all night, you damn well will—or get out. Understand?"

"Yes."

"You can bring the typescript to the morning room when you come into breakfast at seven-thirty."

When he had gone, Jane let out her breath in a gasp and shook her head wonderingly. She must be mad, she decided. No one these days had to work for such a demanding, exacting and dictatorial employer. Why hadn't she told him there and then what he could do with his job? She rubbed her face wearily. Because, she presumed, when he was there, in the same room, the sheer force of his personality overrode all other factors. She simply hadn't thought of doing anything but obey him. He was overbearing and arrogant and she suspected that he could even be cruel; working for him would be no sinecure but at least it would never, never be dull!

She looked at the shorthand notes she had made and for one horrifying moment was sure she could never understand them. Then the cloud cleared from her brain and the symbols began to make sense. She set to work, slowly at first; she had plenty of time really, especially as the typewriter was electric, but she was determined that this first piece of work should be without fault; she had to prove that she was quick witted and efficient and not the bird-brained idiot he no doubt thought her. As she typed and gained confidence, she realised she was typing the chapter of a novel—this part was about a party of six people who seemed to be making their way through a jungle in South America. The Michael Collins style was unmistakeable and she was amazed at how anyone could just rattle off these words, apparently with very little preparation.

She finished typing by seven o'clock, which just gave her time to go to her room, collecting her suitcase on the way, to change out of trousers and into a blouse and skirt, much more suitable for the super-efficient secretary, before taking the typescript along to the breakfast room. She found this room through trial and error only and it was past seven-thirty when she finally stumbled on it. Her employer, now wearing an open neck shirt of navy blue in place of the polo neck jumper, was sitting with Philip. He looked at his watch and said, "You're late!"

"I couldn't find the room," Jane told him, trying to sound cool and placid but not quite able to conceal her annoyance. She placed the papers on the table beside him and turned to go.

"Where are you going?" he demanded authoritatively. "Sit down and have breakfast."

Jane's eyes met Philip's, returning his sympathetic smile. The antipathy she had felt for him vanished as he raised his eyebrows in a comical gesture, as though wondering how she had already managed to get his brother-in-law's back up. Suddenly Philip was a kindred spirit. Jane sat down opposite the two men, folding her hands demurely in her lap.

"I presume you two have met," Carstairs said.

"I collected Jane from the station on Saturday," Philip explained.

"Did you indeed?" There was a wealth of suggestion behind the three small words that Jane, for one, failed to understand. She glanced inquiringly at Philip, but he merely grinned and shrugged his elegant shoulders.

Beth came in then and took their orders for breakfast. When Jane asked for toast and coffee, Max said in a flat voice that brooked no argument, "Miss Murray will have what we have, Beth."

"Yes, sir," the maid murmured and went out. Jane stared across the table at Carstairs, for the

46

first time angry enough to look him straight in the eyes. She experienced a little shock of surprise in seeing that his eyes, that she had thought must be brown, were actually a very, very dark blue, almost navy. They were also, at that moment, amused and she knew he was awaiting her protest. With an effort she lowered her eyes from his and bit back angry words; she was sure she wouldn't come lightly out of an altercation with him and had no wish to be at the end of his biting tongue in front of Philip who was an openly curious spectator. Consequently, she ate her way through the bacon, eggs and tomatoes that were placed before her.

Later, when she was summoned to the library to begin work, she said in a quiet, reasonable voice, "Mr. Carstairs, while I accept that you have the right to dictate my actions as far as my work is concerned, I don't consider you have any right to decide what I eat."

He had been standing by the window looking out and now turned sharply towards her. The left side of his face was in shadow, the scar hidden, and Jane's breath drew in sharply as she watched him. She supposed he must be nearly forty but he didn't look it; when the scar was not in view he looked scarcely different than he had when she saw him at Stratford all those years ago. He had matured of course; his movements were more controlled and his body had lost the colt-like look and was filled out across the chest and shoulders, though he was very fit and athletic looking. He returned Jane's scrutiny, his eyes moving over her as they had earlier, in an impersonal way that was almost insulting because of its lack of interest. Not, she decided hastily, that she wanted him to take an interest in her personally for with his looks and personality he was far too dangerous a man and if he chose a woman as his quarry he would, she was certain, stalk her with the relentless energy of a wild animal hunting its prey.

She shivered in a panicking way at the thought, as he said, coolly, "And suppose, Miss Jane Murray, I choose to disagree with you? I have already told you that I expect you to work hard, very hard, and it doesn't look to me as though you have the stamina. Too many of you young girls these days half starve yourselves to preserve your figures. You need feeding up a bit."

"I'm not a . . . a Christmas turkey!" Jane protested hotly, which made him laugh. "And I do not need feeding up, as you so succinctly put it. I have a perfectly good appetite and do not starve myself. I just don't eat cooked breakfasts. I ate that one this morning because I didn't want to cause a scene, but from now on I'll eat what I want to eat, and short of forcing the food down my throat, there's not much you can do about it!"

She wondered when anyone had last dared to speak to him in this way, and dashed back behind her desk as he took a step towards her. He walked right up to the desk and stood there watching her, gazing steadily into her face until she had no alternative but to look away. Then, just as she was steeling herself against the tirade of abuse that was bound to fall upon her unprotected head, he said, quite calmly, "Very well. You have the right, of course, to eat whatever you wish. Now, shall we get to work, since that is why you are here?" Jane was sure he had deliberately behaved in the opposite way from what she had expected. She could have kicked the man.

They worked through till mid-morning, the time spent mostly by Jane taking dictation. At eleven Sally brought in coffee which was placed on Jane's desk, but Max seemed reluctant to stop work even for one moment. The coffee smelt heavenly and Jane yearned for some, soon deciding that she had better start as she meant to go on. She said politely, "Excuse me, Mr. Carstairs. Do you have milk and sugar?"

"What?" He frowned at the coffee pot as though it were malignant and shook his head. "We haven't time for that."

"I'm sure five minutes won't hurt. We've done a lot this morning. Milk and sugar?"

"Black. One spoonful of sugar," he growled, giving her a fierce glare beneath lowered eyebrows. He had been pacing up and down dictating, not, Jane was relieved to discover, at the furious pace of earlier, though occasionally his voice did gather speed and she was called on to use every bit of her skill. Mostly, though, the pace was reasonable. Sometimes he would pause, hands thrust deep into trouser pockets, brow creased in thought, for anything up to ten minutes at a time and then perhaps ask for something to be read back to him. Once he had shaken his magnificent head angrily and said, "No, that's not right!"

"Perhaps if you . . ." Jane had stopped, horrified at her own temerity, and waited for him to snap at her to look to her own work and leave him to his. He said nothing however and she ventured to suggest in her soft voice, "I was just thinking that if you put that longer descriptive passage— about the alligator, here instead of earlier on, it wouldn't break up the flow of conversation."

He gave her a long considering look then nodded. "All right. Put it there and I'll see how it looks."

Now, as they drank the coffee—and it was real coffee too, not the instant variety—and he lit a cigarette and relaxed at his own desk, he asked, "Have you ever done any writing, Jane?"

The "Jane" thrilled her far more than it should have done and she looked quickly away from him, sure her pleasure must show in her eyes. "I used to write short stories years ago but they weren't much good."

"It's a difficult medium, the short story," he said. "A full length novel is easier in many ways as you have room to develop the characters and plot."

"I suppose so. Did you . . ." she hesitated.

"Did I what?"

"Did you ever do any writing before . . . I mean, it's strange that someone can start just like that, without ever having written anything before. I just wondered if . . ." Jane's voice trailed away into nothing at the expression on his face. Somehow she had stepped over the line and probed too deeply. He didn't look exactly angry so much as bleak, and abruptly he pushed his cup away and said, "Let's get back to work. This afternoon I want you to type all this. You needn't make any copies. Then tonight I'll go through it, making any corrections or alterations. Tomorrow morning you can make the new copies, this time with carbons, and then we'll carry on as we have this morning. Right?" His tone was brisk, cutting off any more confidences or personal touches. Jane had been thoroughly and firmly squashed and she felt a wave of misery sweep unexpectedly over her. She picked up her notebook as he began to speak again.

* * *

This was to be the pattern of her days for the whole of that week. She started getting up very early; the only way to get his alterations re-typed was to do this before breakfast, because immediately after this meal she was expected to take dictation in the library. Often, even during the evenings, he would send someone to fetch her to the library to do more dictation or to type some notes. Consequently, though by the end of that week Jane felt that there wasn't a note in his voice she didn't know and recognise, she knew Max Carstairs the man no better than she had when she first met him. He never again spoke on a personal level.

By the time Philip returned from London on Thursday, Jane was exhausted. He exclaimed at how tired she looked after such a short time and suggested that he take her out for a drive round the New Forest which she had so far seen nothing of.

"We could go to Beaulieu or stop for a meal at one of the pubs in the forest."

"I can't, Philip, I have loads of typing to do," she replied.

"He's a slave driver."

"Maybe. But I have to prove I can work hard. Later perhaps I can relax a bit. Now, please go away, Philip, and let me get on."

Philip's presence made Jane nervous; she knew she was letting the amount of work get on top of her and after only a few days too. Eventually she hoped to be able to persuade Max that he had to ease up on the work he gave her, but just now she wanted only to show that she could do all he required.

"Are you frightened of him?" Philip demanded, and she denied this emphatically. But secretly she rather thought she was a little frightened, or at least wary. He expected her to work as hard as he did himself and God help her or anyone else in his employ who didn't pull their weight. She soon found this out on Tuesday when, having overslept, she was unable to get his altered typescript finished on time. His tongue could lash as effectively as any whip and his training as an actor seemed to help him work himself up into a temper. After that little scene, which had left her shaken, close to tears and feeling physically sick, Jane was determined not to bring his fury down upon her again.

When Jane went to the library on Saturday morning, there was no sign of Max. She caught up on some extra typing and was tidying up her desk when he came in. He was dressed in a charcoal grey three-piece lounge suit and carried a camel-hair car coat over his arm. On seeing Jane he stopped short in the doorway as though surprised to see her there, then he came forward with his usual long, graceful strides.

"My dear child, do you think I intend working you seven days a week?" he drawled lazily. "I shall be away the rest of the day. You can have the weekend off."

"You never said anything," Jane pointed out, a little resentfully, thinking of the warm bed she had forced herself to quit at six o'clock.

"Didn't I? I'm sorry. Would you have gone home?"

"Home? No I wouldn't!" Jane gasped emphatically, having no wish to be anywhere near Isabel.

"You do have a home—parents?" he asked. He had brought a black executive brief case in with him and was in the process of collecting certain things from his desk and putting them into the case. Jane didn't suppose he was really interested in her or her family; he was just asking for the sake of making conversation.

"My father's dead," she told him. "I do have a mother."

"And you don't get on with her."

"What makes you think that?" she asked, surprised.

He sat on the edge of his desk, one long leg dangling, his arms folded across his chest. Jane was struck again by the almost magnetic appeal of him. She had felt it when she saw him on the stage and naturally it was much stronger when he was here, close to her and talking directly to her. If he took the trouble to be kind or charming, as she thought he could be, she was sure no woman could resist him. His looks, of course, were staggering enough without the charismatic appeal behind them. And in some strange way, in Jane's opinion anyway, the scar made him better looking than otherwise. It was as though, without it, he would have been too perfect, which was all very well on the stage or on a movie screen, but not in real life. His features were regular and good, on a classic mould with a marvellous bone structure; his eyes were that unusual dark blue and fringed with lashes as dark as his hair was; that hair, as black as a western European's hair could be, was now streaked with grey at the temples, very distinguished looking and in no way adding to his age; in repose his mouth was beautiful, strongly moulded and mobile though often set in hard, bitter lines as though he didn't like himself, his life or his thoughts very much. Just now the mouth was relaxed; perhaps she had underestimated him and he really was interested in her life.

"You have a very expressive face, Jane," he said, answering her question. "Sometimes, when I do or say something that you consider particularly unjust, the whole gamut of your emotions flies across it—anger, stubbornness, injured innocence. And then I can read your thoughts—shall I tell the bastard what I think of him and his job? No, at least it's interesting and pays well, and it's worth putting up with him for a while." He laughed at Jane's stifled cry of denial. Of course he was, actually, uncannily right. "No, Jane, don't deny it. In my profession—my ex-profession should I say, I learned all about expressing thoughts with one's face. And I agree with you. I *am* a bastard, aren't I?"

"Sometimes," she mumbled, feeling horribly embarrassed and wishing he would drop this awkward conversation.

"Sometimes? Hmmm, how honest you are. Didn't you know an emphatic denial was in order then? How dare you call your employer a bastard."

Jane cried hotly, "I didn't! *You* said it and I merely agreed. You aren't being fair. What do you want me to say—that I do hate working for you, that you are bad tempered and irascible and awkward and . . .?" She bit off her words, horrified, her eyes opening very wide as they met the shock in his. Then she gave a little gasp that was almost a moan and sank back into her chair, her eyes filling with hot tears. Abruptly he moved, reaching out and gripping her chin between thumb and forefinger, forcing her face up towards his. She looked into his eyes, seeing herself -reflected there. A hundred delightful sensations flooded through her at finding herself so close to him; her senses ran wild, each one so alert that she felt his nearness through every pore in her body: the smell of his after shave lotion, the cigars he smoked, the warm, clean masculine body smell. She saw the smooth texture of his skin, the firmness of his mouth, the long curl of his eye lashes veiling his eyes. His fingers hurt her chin and she cherished the hurt.

"Bad tempered, irascible and awkward ... that's what she thinks of me, eh? And she actually has the nerve to say so too. A little slip of a thing young enough to be my daughter ..." he muttered as to himself.

"You'd have to have been a remarkably precocious teenager," Jane replied unsteadily, pulling away from him. She didn't dare look at him again but sat still, staring down at his highly polished black shoes, waiting to be given her dismissal. It didn't come. He remained there for some time, watching her, then he touched her hair lightly and said, "No doubt you're right. But put up with me, Jane, if you can bear to. We work well together, you and I. I've done more work this week than I have for months."

"Have you?" She looked up swiftly, surprising a softened look on his face, a rare, gentle smile that curved his mouth. Then he turned away from her and she watched him pull the car coat on over his suit.

"I'm going to meet my son, Simon, who has been staying with my mother in Scotland. Do you get on well with six year olds, Jane?"

"I've never had much to do with them," Jane

admitted. She got to her feet and walked with him to the front door. "Will you be away long?" she inquired softly and he looked amused.

"I imagine we will be back tomorrow. Why, will you miss me, Jane?"

He took delight in embarrassing her, in watching her too ready blushes and how the colour flooded up over her usually pale face. "It will be very quiet while you're away," she countered, she thought cleverly, and he acknowledged the remark with a laugh.

"I'm not at all sure that was supposed to be a compliment! Goodbye, Jane, till Sunday."

"Goodbye, Mr. Carstairs."

Three

It was ridiculous but she really did miss him. Though life was far from easy when he was there, the house was very empty without him. Jane spent the rest of Saturday catching up on a few personal jobs that needed doing and finally, having put it off all week, she wrote to Isabel. It was a short letter that gave away nothing, certainly nothing about her employer whom she referred to as "Mr. Collins." Max was the sort of man Isabel would be instantly attracted to and Jane wouldn't put it past her to pay her daughter a visit if she knew Michael Collins' true identity.

The time dragged and Jane was pleased to see Philip come in at dinner time, very attractive, gay and openly charming. At least she didn't have to bandy words with Philip. He couldn't embarrass her with a look, or turn her to a stammering schoolgirl with just one word; she didn't need to be on her guard against letting him see how his words and looks affected her. For she had to admit that in one week, Max had worked his way into her thoughts so that he filled them to the exclusion of all others. The strength of his personality was such that no matter how she tried, she could not stop thinking about him and when, over dinner, Philip made some disparaging remark about him, it took all Jane's will power not to shout him down.

"You look a pale shadow of yourself, Jane," Philip told her frankly. "And in only a week. He really does work you hard. The job can't be that important. Why don't you tell him to go to hell?"

"But I don't mind working hard," she insisted. "If the book is going well, naturally he wants to get his thoughts down on paper as quickly as possible. It's really fascinating and, after all, he does pay well in order that I work hard. I'm earning twice as much as I did before."

"You really are becoming his champion, aren't you?" Philip said, dryly. "I hope you aren't doing what I warned you against."

"What's that?"

"Falling in love with him."

"Of course not!" She coloured hotly and looked away in confusion. "Don't be silly. I admire him, of course, both as an actor and a writer, but that's all."

"Because if you are," he went on, ignoring this interruption, "I'm afraid you're in for a shock tomorrow."

"Tomorrow? Why?"

"Because as well as bringing Simon home, he's also bringing Margot." Jane's face was still politely non-committal; probably Max, who was much more discerning than Philip, might have read the hint of wariness in her eyes, but Philip saw only enquiry. "Margot, my darling Jane, is a beautiful, scheming bitch. She looks like a goddess and in front of Max behaves like one. She has one aim in mind, to get Max to the altar. Until recently he's had no serious interest in women.

That's not to say he hasn't had women, of course. After all, Diane's been dead four years and I don't doubt his masculine instincts are as normal as any other man's, but there's been nothing serious. But now he's beginning to get over the bad taste my sister must have left in his mouth and is coming round to the fact that Simon needs a mother."

Jane, whose blushes had been renewed by Philip's outspokenness, said, "Simon—his son," very quietly. She felt suddenly dull and nondescript, a little mouse of a thing who belonged back in the offices of Emerson, Emerson and Marks, where the young, pretty girls would refer to her as "Poor Miss Murray." What was she doing in a world that contained a man like Max Carstairs? What was she doing letting her imagination dwell on how it would feel to be important to him? "Is Simon very fond of Miss Copeland?" she asked, and Philip nodded.

"It's Mrs. Copeland actually. Margot's husband died just before Diane did. Fortunate, wasn't it? Simon certainly behaves better with her than with anyone else. In fact, he's a spoilt little monster who only ever obeys Margot, and Max, of course. He adores Max. With everyone else, including poor Beth, whose job it is to feed him, dress him, put him to bed, et cetera, he does all he can to be as disruptive and rude as possible. He needs a damn good hiding if you ask me."

"But he's only six," Jane demurred. "A little monster at six?"

"You'll see," Philip insisted darkly. "Wait till tomorrow. I bet you'll soon be on the receiving end of Master Simon's dear little ways." He finished his meal and drained his wine glass.

"And now, Jane, since you're free of your lord and master for a whole evening, why don't you and I go out on the town, or, to be more exact since I'm almost broke till the end of the month, out for a drink? Come on, it'll do you the world of good." He put one hand over his heart and smiled brilliantly. "I promise you no more talk of Max, Simon or Margot. Allow me to entertain you, sweet Jane. It will be a never to be forgotten evening—one to warm me in the cold nights to come, when I return to my beastly little flat in town."

Jane laughed and obediently ran to fetch her coat; she was soon sitting beside Philip in his sports car, heading for one of the many large, attractive pubs that abounded throughout the area. It *was* a good evening too. Philip was well-known and liked in this particular hostelry and they were welcomed by a crowd of young people who accepted Jane unquestioningly as one of them. She had never experienced much of a social life and this was her first taste of the company of ordinary young people out for a drink, a game of darts and some decent, friendly conversation. Her shyness was soon banished and she began to enjoy herself. Philip taught her to play darts and she surprised everyone by her steady hand and straight eye. They were two cheerful, happy people who arrived back at Mill House at about eleven-thirty.

"It was a lovely evening, Philip," Jane told him as they went up to the front door.

"We must do it again, next Saturday perhaps," he suggested, searching for his key. "Hell, I've left my key somewhere." He dug about in all the pockets of his sports coat and trousers. "No, I must have left it in my suit."

"What shall we do? We can't wake people up at this time of night," Jane said in a whisper.

"I know. There may be a door or window open. Come on."

They tiptoed round the side of the house, stopping occasionally while Philip prodded in vain at various doors and windows.

"There won't be any open," Jane insisted. "Mrs. Hoskyns is always careful about locking up. If you go on like this, one of the staff will hear and think we're burglars."

"The library," Philip said. "That might be open." He pushed at the French windows and they opened without a sound. The library was in darkness save for a pale glow from the dying remains of the fire. Philip took Jane's hand and they started across the room. By now sheer tension had tightened Jane's nerves to breaking point so that when Philip walked into something, her laughter was let out in an agonised guffaw, echoed by Philip's own.

"Shut up, for God's sake!" he laughed, shaking her.

"I'm t-trying to shut up!" she replied. "Oh, dear, I ache!"

It didn't seem possible that anything could effectively shut off this slightly hysterical paroxysm of laughter, but the one thing that could do it, happened at that moment. The door opened, the light flicked on and Max said, "What the hell is going on in here?"

Laughter was cut off as though a door had been shut on it, though Philip remained cool, grinning cheerfully and saying, "Hi, Max. If I'd known you were about, I'd have rung the door bell so that we could have come in like civilised people instead of creeping about as though we were up to no good. I forgot my key," he explained. "I thought you'd be back tomorrow."

Max had been looking at Jane; she saw how his eyes moved over her, taking in the casual denim trouser suit, her hair tied at the nape of her neck with a chiffon scarf. His eyes were expressionless. She had thought at first that he was angry, and was aware of how tight her breathing had become at the thought of his fury. Yet surprisingly, his indifference was even worse.

"We decided to come back this evening instead," he explained. "Been somewhere special?"

"Only to the White Hart. Er—Margot with you?"

"Yes. We are having a night cap in the lounge. Perhaps you would both join us." There was something in the way he issued the invitation, the silken quality of his voice, that told Jane that the last thing he wanted was for them to accept. But Philip seemed less sensitive and agreed with alacrity.

"I won't, if you don't mind," Jane said quickly, her voice almost non-existent. "I . . . think I've had enough to drink tonight." She glanced up shyly and uncertainly at Max as she passed him but he appeared to look straight through her, stepping out of the way so that she could hurry past. As she set off up the stairs, another door opened off the hall and a female voice—a voice as lovely to listen to in its way as Max's was—low, throaty and perfectly modulated, said, "Max, are you coming back for another drink?"

"Yes, Margot, I'll be right with you," he replied and the door closed again. Jane went on up to her room. She was shocked into numbed incredulity by the fierce intensity of her jealousy.

* * *

Jane slept in late on Sunday morning, missing even her usual toast and coffee. When she finally got up at ten, feeling heavy-eyed and with a headache, she pulled on slacks and a sweater and went downstairs. It was her intention to slip outside so that she could get some fresh air and rid herself of the headache, without meeting anyone. As she passed the library, she heard the typewriter being used in a very slow, uncertain manner and, curiosity getting the better of her, she opened the door softly and peered round it. She was dismayed to find her employer sitting at her desk. As she watched, he made a mistake and swore in a low, angry voice. He looked up and saw Jane standing there, and his black eyebrows snapped together in fury.

"Well, well," he drawled, his voice a soft snarl, "you've finally decided to show yourself, have you? I was beginning to wonder whether I did in fact have a secretary."

Jane walked into the room towards him, bewilderment in her eyes. "But . . . I thought . . . I thought you . . ."

"You aren't being paid to think!" he said icily, his voice ripping her emotions to shreds. "I've been here for hours trying to get this blasted stuff done. Where have you been?"

"I just . . . I just got up," she whispered, and flinched as he thundered, "Just got up! For Christ's sake, it's ten o'clock! Do you think I pay you so you can go out gallivanting half the night and spend the next morning sleeping it off? While I hang around here for hours on end waiting until you deign to rise?"

"That's not fair!" Jane cried, stung into some kind of retaliation at last, though her voice sounded weak and ineffectual beside his. "It's Sunday!"

"I don't recall mentioning when you were employed that you weren't to work on Sunday," he said, no longer shouting but lashing her with his tongue in a way that was far worse than his shouting. "Or did that ridiculous agency that seemed to think I wanted a silly, inexperienced girl as a secretary, dare to set out such conditions?"

She shook her head, unable to speak as tears rushed to her eyes at his cruel, unjust words. She hung her head, biting her lip to keep back that sob that came anyway, a pathetic little sound that in no way assuaged his anger. "Oh, for God's sake don't start crying! That's all I need."

"I'm not crying!" she gulped in a muffled voice that merely proved she was lying. She blinked hard, scrabbling about half-blind until she found note pad and pencil. Eventually, because she simply could not see, she scrabbled round for her handkerchief, sniffing miserably as she looked in vain, and after a moment a handkerchief was thrust under her nose. She took it gracefully and mopped up vigorously. "Thank you."

"Now perhaps we can get on," he said. "Ready?"
"Yes."

Jane met Simon after lunch. To her relief, Max left the library at lunch time, telling her that he was going out to lunch. "Have those notes typed out by this evening," he said curtly. Jane pulled a face at his departing back and wondered whether his exceptionally bad temper was really caused by her or by something quite different. If she was the cause, what had she done? Surely it couldn't have to do with last night, and as for this morning, when he cooled down he would realise how unjust he had been. She heard a car outside and rushed to the window in time to see Max's silver-grey Mercedes just pulling away. Jane glimpsed a passenger sitting beside him.

"Did you see our fair charmer?" Philip remarked, coming into the room and joining her at the window.

"I didn't see her properly." Jane looked up at him. "Was Simon with them?"

"No. He's been left in Beth's care. They've gone to lunch with some people over at Lyndhurst and dear Simon has been left behind. No doubt we'll hear from him before long. He doesn't relish being left out and if he can't make Max and Margot suffer, he'll do his damndest to make us."

"Don't exaggerate, Philip," Jane laughed, but obviously Philip knew Simon quite well for they were only half way through their meal when Mrs. Hoskyns came into the dining room, much distressed and agitated.

"Oh, Mr. Marks, can you come to the kitchen?" she cried. "It's Simon, and I don't know what to do with him. Wrecking my kitchen he is, and when Beth tried to stop him, he kicked her!"

Philip, instead of leaping to help, roared with laughter. "Not on your life, Mrs. H. I've had dealings with that little devil before and I would only be tempted to clobber him." He continued to eat his steak calmly.

Mrs. Hoskyns looked so distressed that Jane felt sorry for her. Almost without thought she put down her knife and fork and stood up. "I'll come, Mrs. Hoskyns."

"You're mad," Philip told her, but she ignored him and followed the housekeeper across the hall, along a narrow corridor and down two steps to the large, modern kitchen. Chaos met her eyes. The floor was littered with smashed crockery and as Jane entered, a cup went flying towards her and smashed on a nearby wall. At her feet lay a plucked, dressed chicken. Directly opposite Jane was the cause of all the trouble, Simon Carstairs, holding in his hands a large earthenware casserole dish as though about to smash it at his feet. His eyes met Jane's and she was conscious of a shock thrilling through her. He was so like his father it was uncanny—the same thick black hair and violet blue eyes; he was a far above-average looking child but just then glared at her in a fiercely aggressive way that robbed him of much of his looks.

"Who are you?" he demanded rudely.

"Jane Murray." She picked up the chicken, and put it on the table. "What a mess in here. Will you help me to clear it up?"

"No, I won't! We've got servants to do that. Who do you think I am?"

"A very rude, ill-mannered little boy."

"You'd better watch out. I'll tell my father about you and he'll get rid of you quick enough. Go away or I'll throw this too."

"Go ahead. It wouldn't bother me since it doesn't belong to me. It must belong to your father I suppose." Jane kept her voice steady and unemotional. It seemed to her that Simon was cursed with a temper to match his father's and, being only six years old and spoiled into the bargain, had no idea how to control it. Just now he was beginning to look uncomfortable, no doubt wishing he hadn't got himself into this situation.

"They shouldn't have gone off and left me!" he cried, suddenly very much a little boy, his lower lip trembling, and Jane's readily sympathetic heart reached out to him. "Not when we only just got back. I haven't seen my Daddy for ages."

"It isn't always easy for grown ups to get out of these kind of things," she explained. "I'm sure your Daddy would have preferred staying with you."

"What do you know about it?" he demanded, and Jane smiled.

"Not much, I admit. But I know he's been working hard all week and going off to a luncheon party is probably the last thing he wanted to do. It's a pity . . ." She sighed and looked round at the mess on the floor. "He'll be awfully upset."

"No he won't. He won't know. It will be all cleared up when he gets back."

"I don't think so. Mrs. Hoskyns, Beth and Sally have lots of other things to do," Jane improvised rapidly. "Perhaps if we started clearing up now . . .?"

"We?" he queried, raising one eyebrow in the same highly imperious gesture that Max used to such advantage.

"You and me."

"I'm not clearing up!"

"Please yourself." Jane shrugged casually and turned to walk away. She wasn't sure that the strategy would work and held her breath, but she hadn't taken more than half a dozen steps before he called her back. At least, he shouted, "Hey, you!" which she didn't object to just then, feeling she had gone quite a long way in one go.

"I can't clean up on my own," he objected.

"No. I'll help. But you must pull your weight."

While sweeping up and getting down on hands and knees beside Simon in order to pick up crockery didn't actually bring her a lot closer to

Max's son, Jane felt that she had at least broken the ice and given herself a chance to get to know him. When they had cleared up she suggested going for a walk and he readily agreed, trotting along quite happily, talking in a remarkably intelligent and mature way, about his day school, his teachers, and his friends. He spoke about some of these people with a frankness that would have been amusing had he not been so young.

"He's stupid!" he said, referring to Philip. "He works for Daddy but half the time he just loafs about doing nothing. My Daddy can't stand layabouts and one day he'll chuck him out."

When Jane made no reply to this comment, he looked up at her, demanding, "Why don't you say something? I'll tell you all about everything if you like. I know lots of things."

"It's none of my business," Jane said, smiling to take the edge off the words.

"The others all wanted to know. The last secretary—great, ugly, fat thing she was—was always asking questions about Daddy. I hated her. I was glad when Daddy got rid of her. He'll get rid of you too if . . ."

"If what?"

"If I decide I don't like you."

"I think your father is more likely to make up his own mind about that," Jane replied serenely, reckoning the only way to get on with this strange child was to stay calm and not take his outrageous remarks to heart. She was feeling rather satisfied with her progress. He wasn't such a bad child after all, and couldn't help being so indulged. Why, Philip had obviously exaggerated how awful he was. Jane smiled down at him and was more than happy when his small hand crept into hers and held it tightly.

This complacency did not last long. Their walk had taken them right round the house and they came to the front again in time to see Max's car draw up and Max and Margot Copeland getting out. Literally before Jane's eyes, Simon changed. A crafty look slid across his still babyish face, making him seem at once adult and sly. He pulled his hand from hers and shouted, "Just you wait and see!" before poking out his tongue and running away. Jane followed more slowly, aware that during the walk she had got herself somewhat dishevelled and even muddy so that her slacks and sweater looked scruffy beside Mrs. Copeland's immaculate green model suit. Margot's appearance was faultless, from the top of her professionally coiffured red head to her high-heeled court shoes; she had the figure of a fashion model to go with her obvious good taste in clothes, and presumably the money to indulge this taste. Jane guessed her to be in her mid-thirties though this impression came more from her obvious assurance and poise than because she looked that age. She looked Jane up and down with open criticism but Jane was too intent on listening in astonishment to what Simon was saying to worry about that just then.

"Oh, Daddy, I'm glad you're back," he cried, his voice shrill and apparently holding back the tears. "She's horrible. She made me clear up in the kitchen after lunch and then forced me to go for a walk in the damp and cold when I wanted to make that model of Concorde you bought me!"

Jane stared, open-mouthed at him, quite unable to believe she had heard correctly, and the child turned huge, innocently bland blue eyes on her so that she almost believed herself to be the brute he had described.

"Is this true?" Margot Copeland demanded in the low, throaty voice Jane had heard the previous evening, and she turned brilliant green eyes upon Jane. "Perhaps you can explain the meaning of such outrageous behaviour." There was a pause then she added, "Who is this . . . person, Max?"

Max had been looking all this time at his son and now he slowly raised his eyes to Jane's face and she experienced the little shock of breathlessness that was beginning to attack her every time he was near. Under other circumstances it was not an unpleasant sensation but just now she could do without it. He looked puzzled and completely ignored Margot's question.

"Perhaps you might care to explain to me what has been going on?" he suggested to Jane.

She took a deep steadying breath. "I think it might be better if Simon told us—all of us," she said. "I think I'd like to know myself."

Simon looked round at the three adults, obviously assessing who would be the most sympathetic, and choose Margot. "It's true, what I said before," he insisted, turning large, limpid eyes upon her. "It is—really and truly."

"Of course it is, darling," she cooed sickeningly. "Don't worry. I believe you, and something will be done about it, have no fear."

"I think," Max said deliberately, "that that is for me to decide, Margot. And I also think we should go inside instead of standing here in the cold." He strode up the steps and in at the front door. Margot, holding Simon's hand, followed. He threw Jane a quick, triumphant look over his shoulder, a look she chose to ignore.

In the hall, Max said, "Margot, would you please take Simon into the lounge and arrange for him to have a warm drink. Miss Murray, come into the library."

Margot looked as though she would like to protest but changed her mind and shrugged, walking off with Simon. Jane, who had been relegated to "Miss Murray," meekly followed Max into the library. It was warm in there and she realised how cold it had been outside. Max crossed and threw another log on to the fire, kicking it into place with the sole of his shoe.

"Now perhaps you'll tell me what has been going on," he said, in a rough, abrupt way. "If you have no objection."

"I don't object, but . . ."

"What?"

"My story is rather different from Simon's and it isn't really important. Can't we just forget it?"

"No we can't!" he snapped. "Good God, you're more of a child than I thought. This isn't a question of telling tales out of school. Simon is difficult, I know, and I have to find out what has been happening."

"He's a spoiled, bad-mannered child," Jane murmured, unable to stop herself saying it. He turned and his eyes flashed.

"That, Miss Murray, is not for you to judge," he said in low, furious tones. "Are you going to give me your version of what has been going on, or am I to believe Simon?"

"Since you obviously believe him anyway, does it matter what I say?"

"Don't be ridiculous, girl!" He was close enough to her now for her to see that he was emotionally disturbed; his eyes seemed darker blue than ever and a little pulse trembled in the scar. As she looked at this, Jane was struck by the most heart-stopping desire to put out one hand and touch it.

Horrified, she dropped her eyes from his face, lest he should read her thoughts as he had before. She gave him a brief, unadorned account of what had happened, cutting it down as much as possible. "I rather think he was upset at being left," she added. "After not seeing you for so long."

"I see. And that is all this is about?" Jane nodded and he continued, "Despite what you think, I do believe you. I'm not a complete fool and I'm aware of how difficult Simon can be. I've always felt that as he has no mother, the loss should be made up to him some other way. It has been difficult to know where to draw the line." His voice trailed away and Jane stole a glance at him, astonished and touched by this brief admission of weakness and possible failure from such an obviously strong man. There was a long silence which she dared not break, feeling closer to him then than she ever had. She was acutely aware of the deep aloneness of him and she longed in some way to give him comfort and help. Then he came out of his meditation and the withdrawn look disappeared to be replaced by the more usual, hard, practical expression. "I'll send him in to apologise," he told Jane.

"No!" Jane cried, chasing after him to the door. "Don't, please. It's unnecessary. Look, I suppose I shall be seeing quite a lot of Simon while I'm here and I've already got off to a pretty poor start. Please leave it and let me try to work it out." His eyes moved slowly over her face as though he would discover her every thought, and she allowed herself a small, tremulous smile. Then he nodded. "Very well, Jane, if that is what you wish."

Four

Apart from her first evening at Mill House, Jane had always eaten her meals with the staff in the kitchen and she assumed that this evening, though Mrs. Copeland and Philip were both staying in the house, that her own eating arrangements would be unchanged. However, at seven o'clock she was summoned to the dining room. Surprised, she obediently changed into a floor-length skirt of a rich claret velvet with a little matching waistcoat, that she had made herself; with this outfit she wore a high-necked white silk blouse, rather Edwardian in style. She twisted her hair round her head in a looser and less severe chignon than usual, and with just a touch of make-up, she had the air of a Victorian—placid, genteel and serene. The outfit suited her, emphasizing her good points; her slender waist and neat, firm breasts, and her pale hair that shone with silver lights. Nevertheless, as she went down to the dining room, she didn't fool herself that she could compete with someone like Margot Copeland.

Opening the lounge door, she was greeted by the sight of Max, very handsome and distinguished in a black dinner suit, standing near the fire talking to Margot. They stood close together, sherry glasses in hands, and Jane heard Max's laughter, soft and genuinely amused. They looked round as Jane came in; Margot was very elegant in a long dress of orange and green silk, bold colours that suited her rather startling colouring. As Jane entered, Max went across to the cocktail cabinet.

"Sherry, Jane? Medium dry, isn't it?"

"Yes, please." Margot's eyebrows rose at this use of Jane's given name. She looked her over with slow contempt and obviously decided she was no threat, for she smiled then, nodding a greeting in a very queenly manner. Max brought Jane's sherry over, handing it to her and saying casually, "Did you object to dining with us, Jane?"

"Should I have?" she countered.

"I thought perhaps you would prefer to avoid us."

"No, Mr. Carstairs," she replied primly. "Though I think it might be more suitable for me to continue eating in the kitchen."

His mouth twitched into silent laughter. It was fascinating to watch the hard lines that were etched round his eyes and mouth disappear for a moment; he looked suddenly much younger and Jane thought this was what he must have been like all the time, before the accident.

"More suitable," he repeated with gentle mockery. "You get more like your namesake every day, especially wearing that very charming outfit."

"My namesake?"

"Who else but Jane Eyre?" he smiled.

"Oh, no!" she gasped, remembering that he had made the most recent film version of *Jane*

74

Eyre. "I hope not. A terrible priggish creature who deserved all she got."

"Oh? What would you have done then, confronted with the fact of Rochester's very much alive wife?" He was trying to embarrass her, and Jane was aware of Margot's resentful eyes upon her, but she would not let herself be embarrassed.

"Oh, I think I would have lived with him unmarried."

"You shock me, Jane. But then, your generation has rather different ideas on such matters than mine."

As he moved away from her, returning to Margot, Jane wondered why he felt it necessary to point out that they were members of different generations. Could it be—and it was a ghastly thought—that he knew how she was beginning to feel towards him and was trying, in a friendly way, to warn her off? To show that to him she was little more than a foolish, star-struck schoolgirl? After all, his stage career must have accustomed him to the adoration of women of all ages. In a way it was true, of course. Sixteen years separated them but it wasn't the disparity in age that lay between them—it was the difference in them as two people, that would always be there even if she were ten years older or he, ten years younger. He was rich, charming, talented, attractive, completely self-assured, and she—she had never in her life been so aware of how ordinary she was. The lovely dream she had allowed herself, that one day he might look at her and discover that she was just what he had been looking for to fill that gap that obviously was in his life, vanished into bitterness as she looked across the dining table into the lovely face of Margot Copeland.

* * *

Jane didn't see Simon again until Wednesday, though she heard him several times, raising his voice at whoever happened to be near at the time—except at Max and Margot, of course. On Wednesday afternoon Jane was working in the library when she became aware that the door had been softly pushed open. Having ascertained the newcomer to be Simon, Jane continued to type and in a little while he walked over and stood watching her fast moving fingers.

"You type fast," he commented seriously. He was holding a pink lollipop and sucking noisily.

"Do I?"

"Much faster than the others. Is that Daddy's new book?"

"Yes."

"I can read it," he said proudly, and proceeded to read the top few lines which happened, fortunately, to be quite unexceptionable material for a six year old.

"That's very good," Jane agreed. "You must go to a good school."

"Pooh! It's awful. They treat us like a lot of babies. My Daddy taught me to read when I was only four."

Jane continued typing. He walked round the desk and stood before her, watching her with large eyes; Jane kept her eyes on her notes, hardly daring to breathe and break the spell. He finished the lollipop and began to touch the things on her desk with gentle, though sticky fingers. Then he said, "You didn't tell my Daddy everything, did you?"

"Everything about what?"

"About the plates—and the chicken."

"Well, by then it was all over and finished with, wasn't it?"

"I'd have told," he declared stoutly. "I think you must be stupid."

"It takes one to find one, chum."

"What does that mean?"

Jane stopped typing. "It means, you have to be a bit stupid yourself in order to know that someone else is."

"I'm *not* stupid!" he began to yell. "I'm . . ." He stopped shouting and suddenly smiled, a remarkably sweet smile, heart achingly like his father's. "Was that a joke?"

"Sort of," Jane agreed with a grin. She started typing again and he said, "I wish you'd stop that and talk to me. No one ever talks to me."

"I'd like to. But I have to finish this by tea time."

"Will my Daddy be cross with you if you don't?"

More than likely, Jane thought wryly, but she said, "No, but I am getting paid and when someone pays you to do a job, then you should do it as well as possible." She had an idea, and dug about in her desk until she found a packet of felt tip pens, a dozen assorted colours, that she had brought with her. She gave them to Simon with a couple of sheets of typing paper. "Why don't you draw something, till I've finished, then I'll talk to you. I won't be much longer."

"Okay," he agreed affably and went to sit at his father's desk, beginning to draw very earnestly, tongue stuck hard in cheek as he concentrated. Jane, looking at the top of his shining black hair, reminded herself that he was only six. He was so intelligent and quick-minded that it was easy to forget that he was really only a baby. Simon glanced up once and caught her eye. "I'm drawing you."

"Are you? It'd better be good."

"It is. I'm a very good draw-rer. Are you a good draw-rer?"

"No, I can't draw anything."

"I can," he said with satisfaction. "You've stopped typing."

"So I have. I'd better get on, hadn't I?"

For a while there was peace save for the soft tap of the typewriter keys and the scrape of the felt tips. Eventually Jane withdrew the final sheet of paper and sorted out her work ready to give to Max. Simon brought over his picture and she duly admired it. He had given the stick-like figure enormous brown eyes and a slightly lunatic smile.

"Goodness. Am I that thin?"

"You are a bit thin," he told her seriously, head on one side as he studied her face and figure. "But I don't mind. Not after the last one. She was fat and she smelt funny." He sniffed hard at Jane, pressing his nose against her shoulder, shedding the last of his animosity and inhibitions as swiftly as only a child can. "You smell nice. Is it perfume?"

"No. Just soap probably."

"Margot smells of perfume. French stuff. It's poohey!" He pulled a comical face and Jane laughed. "Do you like Margot?" he asked.

"I don't really know her very well," Jane hedged.

"She doesn't like you. I heard her tell Daddy he ought to get rid of you. She said, 'She's much too young and will probably make a damn nuisance of herself. You know what these young girls are like, Max.'"

Jane's "Simon, you shouldn't use words like that" came out without thought. Obviously the child was quoting verbatim; he was the sort of lonely child who listened to everything going on around him and wouldn't have made it up. In what way was she "making a nuisance of herself"? Jane frowned and Simon said, "You won't go, will you?"

"I certainly don't intend to."

"I hope you won't. I think I like you after all."

"Thank you, Simon." Jane was inordinately pleased. It was almost as good as if Max had said he liked her; in a way perhaps it was more important than that. There was no doubt that somehow, purely by accident, she had struck the right note in dealing with Simon. He asked, in a polite voice, if he might call her Jane, and did she know any good stories?

"Not stuff like *The Sleeping Beauty* and that. I get fed up with those soppy stories. They never talk about really good stuff. Even in *Red Riding Hood* you never acsherley see the wolf dead with its stomach cut open."

"Blood-thirsty child," Jane smiled.

"Do you know *Rumpelstiltskin*?" he asked. "That's my most favourite of all story."

"I think so."

"Right. You tell me it an' I'll fill you in when you go wrong. Okay? An' can I get on your lap?"

"You're a bit big for that."

"I'm very, very light," he insisted, clambering all over her. They had a brief struggle then got themselves sorted out, with Simon sprawled all over Jane, his arms round her neck. She plunged into the imperfectly remembered *Rumpelstiltskin* and had got part way through when he muttered, his cheek pressed against hers so that she felt his warm breath on her ear, "That's terrible. You've got the story all wrong. I'll tell *you*."

"You do that," Jane said, smiling to herself, and so he did. He was just coming to a magnificent conclusion, illustrating the action with the most blood-curdling shrieks in Jane's ear, when Max came in. Across Simon's shoulder, his eyes met Jane's. He looked so horrified at first that she wondered later if he thought Simon was savaging her or something. But then, realising the situation, his expression softened so much that Jane knew everything would be all right. The deadly atmosphere that had been between them since Sunday was gone. He walked over to her, asking, "Is everything all right?"

Simon twisted round to look at him, surprised but in no way undaunted. "You've spoilt the end, Daddy," he said reproachfully. "I'm just getting to the best part. Ready, Jane? An' then the dwarf was so angry he stamped his foot, an' the foot went right through the floorboards. An' he jumped about, trying to get it out, and screaming all the time like this . . . till in the end he got so *ferorious* he tore himself in half!" He ended on a triumphant note, imitating the dwarf's yells with the most life like shrieks of pain, while Max and Jane looked at each other and smiled.

Max said, "Simon, I believe Beth is looking for you to give you your tea."

"Oh, can't Jane give it to me?"

"No, Jane can't. She is here to help me, not to run round after you. Go on."

"All right," he agreed with a martyred air. He clambered down off Jane's lap. "If you like, I'll tell you some more stories another time," he offered kindly.

"Thank you, Simon. I would like that."

He went out and Jane smiled a little shyly at

Max. "I've finished typing those notes. Here they are."

"It wouldn't have mattered if you hadn't finished," he said softly. "What you have done for Simon—that is far more important. I've never seen him like that with anyone except me. Even with Margot he doesn't completely relax. How did you do it?"

She blushed at the unexpectedness of this praise. "I didn't . . . I mean, he did it. He seemed to want to talk. He's a darling," she added warmly.

"I thought he was a spoiled, bad-mannered child," Max remarked, and she heard laughter on his voice. She returned the smile.

"Yes, he is sometimes. But I don't suppose it's his fault if he's been spoilt."

"Meaning it's mine?"

"Oh, no! I didn't mean that!" Jane felt the heat flush up over her face and cursed this wretched habit of blushing. She once thought she had grown out of it, but since Max's appearance in her life, the annoying, childish thing had resurrected itself.

"If he is spoilt, surely I must be to blame."

"I wouldn't presume to . . ."

"All right, Jane Eyre," he said mockingly. "I was only joking. Don't start getting all uppity with me again." He glanced briefly at the work she had done today. "You can leave the rest of this, Jane."

"All right. Thank you."

She stood up to go, having to brush past him in order to reach the door. Then he called her back. He made her, by the simple expedient of not speaking until she was close to him, walk right up to him so that she couldn't ignore his height or that air of suppressed vitality that he had.

"From now on, take it as granted that you have every weekend off, unless I ask you to do something special. Right, Jane?"

"Yes, thank you." He looked and sounded serious but Jane fancied there was amusement at the back of his eyes, though for once she was sure he wasn't laughing at *her.*

"Don't thank me. It's a right. I'm not very good at apologising, Jane, and even now I'm three days late, but I do beg your pardon for being, not only unjust, but inexcusably rude and bad-mannered."

"Oh, no!" Jane whispered faintly, overcome by the sheer unexpectedness of the apology. "You had the right . . ."

"No, Jane. I had no rights. Do you forgive me?"

She nodded, so embarrassed that she could only mutter at his feet, "Is that all?" and when he said it was, she made her escape hastily, leaving him standing there watching her.

It seemed that Jane had found not only a friend in Simon but also a disciple. During the weekdays he was at school but the moment he arrived home at three-thirty he would break away from Beth who fetched him from his prep school and come running to the library where Jane would inevitably be working. She didn't know the reason for this devotion but made a shrewd guess that he sensed, as children often can, that Jane liked him for himself and not, as Margot did, for an ulterior motive. Simon was perhaps too young to put his feelings into words but it was possible that he knew Margot was kind to him only because she wished to please Max.

Jane began to re-organise her work so that she was able to give Simon her time when he came

home. Max seemed to realise that she was doing
this and, though nothing was ever said, he cut
down her work so that she was able to finish most
days by four. Max obviously appreciated the
change in Simon; in less than a fortnight this
change was very noticeable. He tagged along
behind Jane like a puppy, invariably friendly and
hardly ever having one of his screaming fits.
Because Margot had left after a few days, life was
easier and happier for Jane. She had been at Mill
House five weeks now and her past life had
receded into insignificance. She never thought
about her previous job, or Miss Parsons and the
other girls at the office. She had even forgotten
about Isabel's marriage until a post card arrived
one morning from Malta where Isabel and Malcolm were honeymooning. Max handed her the
postcard at breakfast, which they ate together in
a fairly companionable silence. Jane chewed her
toast and surreptitiously watched Max's long
fingers, adorned only by the heavy gold signet
ring on his right hand, as he sorted out the mail
and handed over the postcard. "You have friends
in exotic places, Jane," he remarked in his beautiful, lazy voice, the voice that never failed to send
shivers of delight down Jane's spine no matter
how often she heard it. She took the post card
and read the brief inscription.

"It's from my mother," she said. "She's on her
honeymoon."

Naturally this remark required some explanation. His eyes remained steadily on her face as she
told him about Malcolm Harris and she had the
eeriest feeling that he understood everything. He
said, "So that's why you wanted this job, to escape
your mother and her new husband. Don't you get
on with them?"

"I enjoy the job!" Jane said hastily. "I don't stay because I have nowhere else to go!"

"Answer my question then, or tell me it's none of my damn business."

"I don't get on very well with Isabel, my mother," Jane admitted. "We never did like each other very much. Isn't that awful?"

"I don't see why people should be duty bound to like the members of their family."

"I used to feel very wicked, because sometimes I hated Isabel. And she never really pretended to like me. She should have had a pretty little girl with curly hair and blue eyes who she could dress up in frilly clothes and show off to her friends. I was never like that. I used to hate being dressed up and I always said the wrong things at her horrible tea parties."

He smiled. "What about your father?"

"Oh, he was different. I loved him." Jane sighed, staring ahead of her as she wandered in her mind back over the years. "I don't think their marriage can have been very successful. Goodness knows what they saw in each other. I don't remember them arguing but then, I don't remember them talking either. I suppose, when he died, Isabel and I just went on living in the same house through habit."

"And your stepfather?"

"Oh, he's . . . well, maybe it's just me. I don't like him."

"Because he has taken your father's place?" Max suggested and Jane shook her head vehemently.

"I couldn't care less who Isabel married. They're welcome to each other. But I couldn't stay in the same house with him." She shuddered eloquently so that it didn't take a lot for someone as perceptive as Max to guess the cause of her dislike of Malcolm Harris.

"He made a pass at you!" he guessed triumphantly, and Jane nodded.

"Yes, he did. Several passes. I didn't seem able to get it into his thick head that I couldn't stand him, and if I'd told Isabel, she would have said I encouraged him. She wouldn't believe," Jane said a little bitterly, "that he could possibly look twice at *me*."

Max, elbows on table, chin resting in his cupped hands, watched her with a contemplative smile lurking about his mouth and Jane, realising she had gone on far more than she should have, blushed and looked away from him. He said, his voice slightly husky as though with held back laughter, "You should be firmer, Jane. Most men can be handled if you only know how." He saw her confusion and stood up, collecting his mail together and saying, enigmatically as he walked out, "I hope you don't consider you've stepped out of the frying pan into the fire, Jane."

"How was school?" Jane asked Simon when he came in that afternoon. It had been snowing since lunchtime and he was very bright-eyed with pink patches on cheeks and nose.

"Rotten. They wouldn't let us go out to play in the snow." He sighed, leaning on her desk. "You're not still working, are you? I thought we could go and look for tracks. My teacher says you can see all sorts of things in the snow—birds' and animals' feet prints and things like that. Can you come?"

"Sorry, love, but I must finish this. I'll be about an hour."

"It'll be dark by then!" he objected.

"Perhaps Beth will take you out."

"She wouldn't go walking in the snow. She moaned just bringing me home. An' anyway, she doesn't know things like you do." He sighed heavily before straightening himself off the desk and walking out, presumably to pester someone else. Jane continued with her work but interruptions were not over with, for he was soon back, this time with Max in tow.

"It's all right, Jane," he yelled. "Daddy says you can leave all that!"

"Simon!" she reproved. "You shouldn't have . . ."

"Don't worry, Jane," Max smiled. "I'm sure, if you don't mind, that a walk will do you both good." The sight of him had, as usual, left Jane breathless and confused, uncertain and not quite in control of her limbs. She detested this weakness and hadn't yet got round to analysing its cause, but she wasn't up to arguing. She covered the typewriter and went upstairs to change into slacks, boots and a warm jacket. When she came down, Simon and Max were both in the hall, Simon all wrapped up in a fur-lined anorak, hood pulled up round his small, excited face, his long trousers tucked into Wellington boots. Jane hardly noticed this, however, for her eyes were on Max, who also was dressed to go out, in a dark-grey duffel coat and boots.

"Daddy's coming too!" Simon yelled as she came into view.

"Do you mind, Jane?" Max asked softly.

"Of course not," Jane murmured in reply and, because she could not tell him how pleased she was, she added, "I could hardly object to you walking in your own grounds, could I, Mr. Carstairs?"

She couldn't explain the look that flashed over his face as she spoke. It wasn't anything definite—annoyance, or exasperation, or any similar emotion. There was just a flickering at the back of his eyes that might almost have been pain, only that, of course, was ridiculous. Why should anything she said matter to him? But because she was confused and wished she had held her tongue, she pushed past him and went outside.

The wind, the cold and the driving snow hit her all at once and Jane gasped. Next moment a little whirlwind that was Simon had grasped her hand, pulling at her, and he and Jane were running across the lawn, laughing and yelling. By the woods they stopped and got involved in a little screeching horseplay, throwing snowballs at each other, while Max caught up with them. Jane was aware of his tall, broad-shouldered figure silently watching them, an indulgent smile on his face, as though they were both children. Then Simon threw a snowball at his father and next moment Max had joined in too. His aim being so much better than theirs, his ability to dodge also, he came off lighter than either of them. They were a lovely few minutes, Jane guessed the most carefree Max had spent in years. It was wonderful to hear him laugh without restraint, to see him lift Simon high in the air while the child shrieked with delight and the snow flurried round them.

It all ended rather unexpectedly when Jane went flat on her face in the snow and Simon, carried away by the snow and the joy of having his father with him, threw himself upon her and before she could stop him had stuffed a fistful of hard-packed snow down her neck.

"Oh, Simon, you little wretch!" she yelled, pushing him off and sitting up, trying to get the snow out before it melted. Max, laughing, came over and helped her to her feet.

"Keep still," he ordered, "and put your head forward."

Jane did as she was told and felt him digging his hand down the back of her neck, under her coat and jumper, and retrieving most of the snow before it could do more than make her rather damp. Then he took out his handkerchief and gently wiped her neck. Only then did Jane become aware of how they were standing, his left arm round her waist, holding her hard against him, and her head bent forward, resting on his shoulder. Despite the thick clothing they both wore, it seemed as though she could feel the hard leanness of his body against hers and the tense strength of his arm about her. She was suddenly struck by the foolish notion that she wouldn't have minded being held like this for a good deal longer. With this thought she panicked and would have moved away, but his arm tightened, holding her a moment longer and she dragged her head back, looking up into his face. There was snow on his eyelashes and on his thick, black hair and his mouth turned up into a faint smile before he released her.

"No more rough stuff, Simon," he said, and there was a sweet, husky note in his voice that Jane knew she hadn't imagined. She turned away quickly and walked on, hands deep in coat pockets, shaken rigid by the short episode. She was being silly, getting an obsession about a man who could never be for her. She had no more sense than that foolish ten-year-old girl who had once put his pictures all over her bedroom wall. Why, when she wasn't actually working with him, he treated her as he did Simon, as though she

Step out of your world and enter

CIRCLE OF LOVE

the Circle of Love.

Treat Yourself to a New Romance

A new romance is just what you need. A Circle of Love romance. They're better-written romance novels, *full of intriguing men. Exciting international locales. Fantasies of never-ending love.*

Circle of Love romances are unlike any romance novels you've ever read. They're more compelling, more absorbing, and more satisfying page after page.

Receive the Next Six Titles Absolutely FREE

Now you can receive the next six Circle of Love romances absolutely free. It's your introduction to the Circle of Love Reader's Service. Just send in the card at right. Then we'll rush you the next six *all-new* Circle of Love titles. They're yours to keep whether or not you decide to continue the Reader's Service monthly program.

But if you enjoy the great reading, the convenience of home delivery, and *no* postage and handling charges, you can continue your membership simply by paying $10.50 for each shipment of six romances. You can even have each month's shipment of six titles charged automatically to your VISA or Mastercard account each month when it is shipped.

So don't miss next month's titles. *Send no money now.* But mail the postpaid card today.

Dear Reader:

With all the romance novels available, finding consistently satisfying reading is still not easy.

In Circle of Love romances, you're assured better writing. The stories are more suspenseful and more realistic. The characters are more genuine. And the romance is more satisfying from beginning to end.

Now you can enter the Circle of Love each month with the convenience of this no-risk offer.

Cordially,

Cathy Camhy

CATHY CAMHY *for Circle of Love*

Membership Application

☐ **YES.** Please send me FREE and without obligation the next six Circle of Love romances. Then send me the next six together with an invoice for $10.50. There are no charges for shipping and handling. The first six books are mine to keep whether or not I decide to continue my membership. There is no minimum number of books that I must buy, and I may cancel my membership at any time.

SIGNATURE _____

NAME _____

ADDRESS _____

CITY _____ STATE _____ ZIP _____

Payment Options: (check one)

☐ Charge each regular shipment to my: ☐ Bill Me

      13011 ☐ Mastercard   ☐ VISA   11015

_____

(Credit Card Number)   *expiration date*

Send no money now--but mail today

This offer is good only in the U.S.   C 12

BUSINESS REPLY MAIL
FIRST CLASS   PERMIT NO. 2226   HICKSVILLE, N.Y.

Postage will be paid by addressee:

Circle of Love

READER'S SERVICE
Bantam Books
P.O. Box 994
Hicksville, N.Y. 11802

and his son were the same age. She had to stop this nonsense before it even started.

After searching in vain for animal tracks in the snow, Max announced that it was time they got back. Philip came out of the library as they got inside, having stripped off their wet, outer clothing in the porch and left everything to drip. Looking extremely elegant in a blue suède jacket over a pale blue silk shirt and dark slacks, Philip regarded Max with astonishment, then looked at Jane. There was a thoughtful look on his face as he walked over to her and, to her astonishment, kissed her cheek.

"You look gorgeous, Jane darling," he said, giving her a hard squeeze before she could escape. "The cold has put beautiful colour into your cheeks. I'm very glad I decided to stay on a few more days. What say you and I drop round to the White Hart this evening for that meal I promised you?"

Jane decided to ignore the "darling." She couldn't remember a meal having been mentioned but didn't like to say so, not in front of Max, and Beth, who had just come from the kitchen and was in the process of relieving Simon of his boots and wet socks. So she smiled noncommittally, thinking it would be easy enough to get out of the evening later. Then Max said, in a peculiar, flat sort of voice, "Don't be a fool, Philip. You can't go driving about the forest in this weather. It's blowing up a blizzard."

Philip shrugged. "What do you say, Jane?"

Jane didn't much care to say anything, so she jumped at the excuse Max had presented to her. "It's pretty ghastly out, Philip. Perhaps some other time . . ."

"As you say, love. The weekend maybe. We could

go into Southampton perhaps, take in a show and dance afterwards." It sounded like a long evening, too long, but Jane wasn't up to arguing just then. Besides, she couldn't help wondering what Philip was up to, with this sudden rush of affection. He was behaving as though they were far closer than they actually were. She escaped before he could say anything more, and set off up the stairs, aware of them all standing there watching her departing back.

Dinner that evening was awful. Simon had been allowed to make up the foursome and he alone seemed unaware of the atmosphere that to Jane just couldn't be ignored. Max was at his worst, making nasty little biting comments at her, things that in themselves seemed unimportant but the way he said them—and he certainly knew how to put a barb into the most harmless remarks—really hurt. Once he said, his voice as cold and bitter as the wind that even then howled round the house, "What are you doing for Christmas, Jane?"

She stared blankly at him. "Christmas?"

"It is only three weeks away," he told her. "I suppose you'll want to go home. People usually want to be with their families at Christmas, don't they?"

This was deliberately cruel as he knew very well how things were with Jane and her family. She looked steadily at him, hoping to find some trace of shame in his eyes, but they were blank and in the end she was first to turn away.

Then he said, "Of course, I don't suppose you'd be very welcome, would you?" He turned to Philip and said, as casually as if he were making a remark about the weather, "Jane's mother loathes her and her step father can't keep his hands off her. It sounds like a plot for a modern television play, doesn't it?"

"Max!" Even Philip was shocked by this, and Jane lifted her eyes to him. "Don't worry, Philip. It's quite true. I can assure you it doesn't bother me in the least if . . . if someone wishes to talk about my . . . my private life." Her voice, suddenly very young, faltered slightly and her pain was lightened, not by Max but by his son.

"I want Jane with us at Christmas, Daddy."

"Jane won't be able to be with us," Max said, his tone still flat. "We are going to London for Christmas."

"That's the first I heard of it," Philip remarked.

"I was not aware that I had to report my every decision to you, Philip," Max replied.

Jane's unhappy eyes met Philip's across the table and his eyebrows rose as though he too wondered what had brought on this foul mood. Jane thought of Max as he had been earlier in the snow, laughing and youthful and carefree; she thought of his gentleness as he got the snow off her. How could a man change so? She did not understand him at all and was now so frightened of bringing his wrath down upon her head again, frightened in case next time she would not be able to hold back the tears, that she didn't speak again but ate her dinner in silence.

Then Max said, his tone still somehow insulting, though Jane couldn't have said exactly *why* it was, "You can stay here if you want to. The staff will stay on and I daresay there will be some form of festivities. And I can always give you some research to do."

Their eyes met again, and again Jane looked away first, not wanting him to see how much he hurt her. But she had no choice in the matter and, though she didn't relish spending Christmas ploughing through books looking for bits of information for him, she nodded. "Thank you," she murmured.

"You can't do that, Max!" Philip interrupted. "I never heard anything like it in my life, expecting the poor girl to stay down here and work all the time! It's damned unfair!"

"I wish you would learn to mind your own business, Philip," Max said, his voice heavy with boredom. "She happens to be merely an employee, not my guest."

This insult was pointed and so obvious and painful that Jane could not quite restrain a gasp. Philip too looked shocked, finally finishing his wine with a gulp and standing up. "Excuse me," he said quietly. "I'm going into the lounge. Jane, how about a game of chess?"

She glanced at Simon, tucking into his ice cream and apparently unaware of what had been going on, and at Max who was gazing into the red depths of his wine glass and seemed oblivious to their existence, and nodded, following Philip out. They were both silent as he set out the chess pieces, then she said uncertainly, "What's happened, Philip, to put him in such a terrible mood?"

"Don't you know?" he asked.

"No. Do you?"

He looked thoughtfully at her, then smiled a secret little smile that said much though not in any language that Jane understood. "I'm not sure," he murmured, "But I'm beginning to wonder. Your move, Jane."

There was no sign of Max that evening and soon Jane went to bed, leaving Philip alone in the lounge. She had a headache and took a couple of aspirins, hoping that she would soon sleep. But though the aspirins cured the headache, sleep proved to be elusive. Somewhere in the house a clock struck midnight and she was no nearer sleeping than when she came to bed. She decided to read for a while—she still hadn't finished *Ice Fall*, which she had bought before coming to Mill House—and she sat up, putting on the light and getting out of bed to look for it. Then she remembered that she had taken it downstairs to read when she was having her mid-morning coffee. After ten more sleepless minutes she decided there was nothing to be done but to go and fetch it. The house was in darkness and it was unlikely she would meet anyone, so she wrapped herself up in her modest yellow quilted dressing gown, belting it firmly round her middle, and slipped on her slippers before creeping softly along the gallery and down the oak staircase to the hall.

There was still a good fire burning in the library, lighting the big room with an eerie, flickering light that illuminated it enough for Jane to see the book on her desk. She walked over to it and had just taken the book between her fingers when a voice said, "What are you doing here?" Jane shrieked and dropped the book with a bang that seemed inordinately loud in the large, dark room. There was a movement by the fire and then the standard lamp was switched on and she saw Max. He was sprawling in his big leather chair, legs stretched out before him, dark head resting against the wing. In one hand dangled a cigar and in the other a whisky tumbler. Jane's swift glance took in the half empty decanter on the small, side table at his elbow. She noticed that he also was dressed for bed, in dark red pyjamas beneath a bottle green dressing gown. Only when he spoke, repeating his original question, did she also suspect that he was drunk, or at least getting on that way. His voice had lost its usual drawl; it was quickened, rather clipped, as though he forcibly controlled it.

"I . . . I came down for a book," she managed to reply, bending to pick up the novel. "I couldn't sleep."

"Nor I. Though my remedy seems rather more drastic than yours." He held out one hand and Jane obediently placed the book in it. He glanced at the cover and laughed harshly, not a pleasant sound. "How very loyal of you, Jane. But then, you are, aren't you? The loyal little secretary who never puts a foot wrong, never disrespectful, or bad tempered."

"I don't know what you mean," she said softly, taking the book back from him. She stood watching him gravely, a small, slender figure in the yellow dressing gown, her eyes huge in her pale face, her long silver hair a shining halo round her head and shoulders.

"No, I don't suppose you do," he said, taking in her appearance in a single glance. "Oh, go away, Jane!"

His tone was sharp and she turned, walking swiftly away from him, only to be brought up sharply by his calling of her name. She looked round just as he stood up and came towards her. He said, "I'm sorry. I didn't mean that. Come and sit down for a while."

She shook her head. "No, thank you. I'll go back to bed."

"Come and sit down," he insisted, tightening his fingers round her arm and pulling her forcibly back to the fire. She went with him but refused to sit down. He tipped some whisky into another glass and handed it to her and she sipped the liquid a little distastefully but unwilling to antagonise him further. He stood before her, staring at her in a way that was both disconcerting and embarrassing.

"Is anything wrong, Mr. Carstairs?" she asked, and he started as though he had not been seeing her at all, but had been lost in his own thoughts. Then he said harshly, "Will you stop calling me "Mr. Carstairs" in that prim and proper way? My name is Max! Say it!"

"I don't think I . . ."

"Say it!" he demanded fiercely. "Max! Say it!"

"Max."

"That's better." He sounded a little more reasonable now and Jane thought she might make her retreat. She was more than a little frightened of him in this strange mood, yet also reluctant to leave him. It was as though a thin thread of elastic stretched between them so that no matter what he did or said, she was pulled back to him. The truth was, she supposed, she wanted to be with him, no matter what. She handed the whisky glass back to him.

"I don't want any more, if you don't mind."

"Suppose I do mind?"

"Then I'll drink it."

"I believe you would. Always so obedient, aren't you?"

There was mockery on his face and in his voice, and for the life of her Jane couldn't resist saying, "As you yourself said, Mr. Carstairs, I am your employee, not your guest."

"Ha! That annoyed you, did it? I wondered what it would take to get through that cool, placid exterior."

"It didn't annoy me, but . . ."

"What?"

"It hurt," Jane admitted quietly and heard his breath being drawn in sharply. She wasn't looking at his face but in the general direction of his chest, but she saw his hand move and felt it rest lightly on her hair, slowly stroking it. Jane closed her eyes, hardly daring to breathe, her heart hammering uncomfortably. She felt rather than saw that he had come closer and she couldn't move. It was as though all this was happening to someone else, as though she stood outside herself and watched. Time moved swiftly and inexorably towards the only possible conclusion. His hand forced her chin up and she opened her eyes and looked into his. She could smell whisky on his breath but strangely it wasn't unpleasant.

"You should always wear your hair like this," he murmured, his breath warm on her lips. "You look like my wood nymph again . . . Jane." Then he was kissing her, slowly and gently at first, his lips as soft and sweet as she could ever hope for, while his fingers stroked her neck and shoulders lightly beneath the collar of her dressing gown. Then it wasn't gentle at all; she was pulled hard against him, and for a moment she struggled in the face of a force and a rush of desire that she did not understand. But it was useless to struggle and soon she had no wish to struggle anyway. She wrapped her arms round his neck, allowing her lips to open under his, tasting the sweetness of his mouth, drowning in her longing for him. His hand pulled at the belt of her dressing gown and it fell open so that only the double layer of nylon was between her soft skin and his hands. She shivered with the prickles of delight his touch roused in her and he in return pressed himself harder and closer to her so that they seemed to fuse into each other.

Then a shudder went right through him and he caught at her shoulders, pushing her away as though her arms had been imprisoning him. She fell back hard against the armchair and he turned away from her, his body stiff, his hands to his head. She heard him gasp, "My God, what am I doing?" in an agonised voice.

Uncertainly she whispered, "Max?" and he shook his head and turned to look at her.

"Christ, girl, don't you know anything? Haven't you more sense than to let a man—a man you hardly know—touch you like that?"

Bewildered, she shook her head wordlessly and watched his anger fade. She was not frightened of him and knew that his fury was directed against himself. He came back to her and with great gentleness pulled her dressing gown back round her and re-tied the belt. She watched him worriedly, impulsively lifting her face a little. Their eyes met and with a little groan he bent his head, resting his mouth on hers, close-lipped and without passion.

"Go to bed, Jane," he muttered, holding her against him for a short, sweet moment. She heard him whisper into her hair, "I'm drunk, that's all . . . don't know what I'm doing. I'll have forgotten all this in the morning and you would do well to do the same. Do you hear me, Jane?"

"Yes."

"Max."

"Yes, Max."

"Goodnight then, Wood nymph."

"Goodnight, Max." His lips brushed lightly across her forehead and she moved away, leaving him standing there, very still, staring into the flames. She looked back and thought how lonely he seemed to be; she longed to return to him. But she didn't. There were some things a girl like her couldn't do.

Once back in her own room, Jane sat before the dressing table staring at herself in the mirror. Her colour was heightened and her mouth still soft and crushed by his kisses; the pale oval of her face swam before eyes that were filled with sudden hot tears. She blinked fiercely as she took her brush and began to brush her hair with hard, brisk strokes that made her scalp tingle. Forget it, he had said. He would have forgotten in the morning and she would do well to do the same. Forget that for a few minutes she had attracted him, he had wanted her. Forget she had been held in his arms and kissed with tenderness and with passion. How could she ever forget the visions of delight his embrace, his kiss had opened out for her? How could she pretend it had never happened?

"I love him," she whispered to her reflection, and knew then that this love had been building up for the last few weeks, perhaps from the moment she had met him. She said slowly experimentally, "I love Max Carstairs."

Why it was she didn't know, but the speaking of his name made her feel better. She smiled briefly to herself and took off her dressing gown, slipping into bed. The sheets had grown cold and she shivered for a while until her body warmth overcame the chill. Then she snuggled down and closed her eyes. At least she was here, in his house; at least she was able to help him in his work and she had learned to know and love his son. Perhaps, if she always worked well, he would let her stay on with him. After all, there would be other novels and he would always need a secretary.

With martyr-like visions of giving her life to him, so that when she was old she would be able to look back over years of faithfully serving the man she loved, Jane finally slept.

Five

The local amateur dramatic society were doing the pantomime *Cinderella* for Christmas and Jane had the idea of taking Simon. Subtle questioning revealed that he had never seen a pantomime and though he professed to dislike "soppy fairy stories," she was sure he would enjoy this. During the afternoon following the incident with Max in the library—it had to be termed an "incident" for he had greeted her quite normally the following morning—she found time to slip into the village to buy the tickets. They were on sale in the village post office and Miss Gibson, the postmistress, was delighted to see Jane. On other occasions, when Jane had been in there, she had had difficulty in avoiding questions fired at her by the inquisitive little spinster. Miss Gibson was harmless enough but she was extremely curious and also, as she now revealed to Jane "one of Mr. Carstairs' most devoted fans." It was no secret to anyone in the village who the owner of Mill House was, and Max's presence in and around the village was accepted as a matter of course.

"Really?" Jane said noncommittally.

"Yes indeed. Such a talented man, so handsome too, and that beautiful voice! When my sister Gladys was alive, we often went to Stratford or to London, just to see him on the stage. I think his Mark Antony was my favourite—such a romantic play, but I also had a particular fondness for his Richard III. So amusing."

"Amusing?" Jane queried. Amusing was the last word she would have used to describe Shakespeare's Richard III.

"Oh, yes. He played it very tongue-in-cheek. I believe there is a theory that Shakespeare intended it played like that, not grotesque and wicked as it is usually done. He wasn't really like that, you know."

"Who wasn't like what?"

"Richard III. He wasn't a hunchback or ugly and he didn't go round murdering people either. Henry VII had those stories put about to blacken his name."

"Yes, I've heard that." Before Miss Gibson could say more, Jane quickly went on to ask for two tickets for the pantomime.

"Of course, dear. Any particular evening?"

"I gather it starts on New Year's Day. Any time will do."

"The first night is when the old-age pensioners are invited free of charge. Would the following day be all right?"

"Fine." Jane handed over the money and quickly made her escape. She looked forward to telling Simon about the pantomime. It seemed to her that the boy had little enough fun in his life. Jane didn't blame Max, but a man could never completely fill a young child's life. He saw that Simon's physical needs were satisfied, that he was educated and clothed and fed, but Simon needed a woman's love and caring. At least as long as she, Jane, was at Mill House, Simon could have a taste of that kind of love. To be able to help Simon and make him a little happier would at least partly assuage the ache of longing she felt for Max.

Reaching the gate of Mill House, Jane set off up the drive. She looked critically at her surroundings. The gardens would look lovely if they were cared for—she might even have a go at the roses herself. Most of them were only in need of a pruning. She paused on a bend in the drive, looking beneath a beech tree, where some snowdrops were already forcing their way up through the snow that still covered the ground. She crouched down and gently pushed the snow away from the tiny green shoots.

"There you are, that'll give you a better chance," she murmured, and straightened up, continuing her walk.

A pale blue Rover that Jane didn't recognise was drawn up outside the house. She glanced at it with curiosity as she went round to the back entrance by the kitchen.

Mrs. Hoskyns was in the kitchen making pastry; the most delicious smells pervaded the atmosphere and Jane sniffed appreciatively as she put her head round the door. "Some thing smells good."

"That's my Christmas cake," Mrs. Hoskyns said, looking pleased. "It's a bit late but I wasn't going to make one. Now, seeing as you'll be here as well as me and the hubby and Sally too, because her Dad's in the army and the family is in Germany, I thought I'd do something special."

"If it tastes as good as it smells, it'll be lovely," Jane said, going into the kitchen. "Who does the blue Rover belong to?"

"That's Mrs. Copeland's," Mrs. Hoskyns said,

kneading the pastry with skill and energy. "Came down on her own about an hour ago."

"Oh! I didn't know—I mean, Mr. Carstairs didn't mention it."

"I don't expect he knew, Jane. Comes and goes, she does, whenever she feels like it, and always welcome of course, her and Mr. Carstairs being so close."

"Oh! I didn't know . . ." Jane repeated in a hollow voice. She thought about Margot Copeland's sophisticated beauty. She was the ideal sort of woman for Max.

The housekeeper smiled cheerfully, unaware of the pain she was giving to Jane. "You wouldn't, would you, dear? Funny, they are, making out there's nothing between them—but I know. Why, only a little while ago, just before you came it was, I saw them in the library together, kissing they were. Well, I say it's a good thing. She's a real lady, is Mrs. Copeland, and she'll make him a good wife. It's time he thought about getting married again. This house needs a mistress and Simon, a mother."

Jane chewed the currant bun Mrs. Hoskyns had given her and it tasted awful, like ashes, and was thankful that the older woman was too busy with her apple pie to notice her dismayed jealousy at the thought of Max and Margot. "I expect it would be a good thing," she murmured and left the kitchen. She hung up her coat and went out into the hall intending to go up to her room.

She had taken only a few steps when a commotion from the direction of the lounge stayed her steps. A high pitched scream was followed by Simon's shrill voice. "No, I won't! I won't!" A moment later the door opened and Simon came shooting out, still yelling. Catching sight of Jane, he hurtled across to her, launching himself into her arms and clinging round her neck. He was not crying but his body shook and shuddered as he held on to her.

"Simon, what is it?" Jane asked, holding him easily in her arms. He didn't answer directly but repeated, "I won't do it! I won't!"

Across his head, Jane saw Max come from the lounge, a very angry looking Max who said, "Simon, come here. You will apologise to Mrs. Copeland at once!"

Simon's body shook convulsively as his hold on Jane tightened. She looked at Max. Hands on hips, feet slightly apart, he looked very aggressive and it was hard to imagine what Simon could have done to cause this rage. He said, more quietly, "Put him down, Jane. He is old enough to face trouble. Simon, come on!"

"What has he done?" Jane asked.

"That doesn't concern you." Max strode over to her, forcibly extricating Simon from her arms and setting him on his feet. Jane looked up into his implacable face and then at Simon, who stood between them, hands clenched into tiny fists, his mouth set hard. Under other circumstances it would have been funny. They were so alike. Even this aggressive stubbornness was the same.

Max took Simon's hand and dragged him back into the lounge, and Jane followed. It took only a cursory glance to see what was amiss.

Margot Copeland stood in the middle of the room, outrage and fury on her lovely, flawless face. As usual, she was immaculate, her beautifully coiffured hair, her make-up, the russet brown woollen suit all perfectly attuned. The ink stain, fair and square on the front of the jacket, emitting long trails of black ink down to the skirt, was an outrage. Jane felt her eyes pop and her breath caught in dismay at what Simon had done.

"Now, Simon, your apology," Max said quietly.

"I won't! She asked for it!"

"Simon!" Max bellowed. At the same time, Margot snapped, "Really, Max, this is ridiculous. The child is little more than a wild animal. He is hopelessly spoilt." Obviously the charm she usually reserved for Simon when Max was present was sorely tried by this assault upon her person and she was unable to keep up the pretence. Max threw her a look scarcely less vicious than the one he had given his son. Despite this, Jane felt suddenly sorry for him. He was such a strong man, yet now he seemed unable to handle the situation. Impulsively, she went over to Simon, crouching before him.

"Say it, darling," she murmured softly, for his ears alone. "It won't hurt and you know you must apologise. No matter what the reason, you shouldn't have done it."

The mutinous look faded. "Are you cross too?"

"No, Simon, I'm not cross."

"All right." He turned to Margot and took a deep breath. "I'm sorry I threw the ink at you," he said in a falsetto voice. Then he spoke to his father and for the first time a sign of weakness crept into him; his lips trembled. "Is that all right?"

Max nodded, his expression gentling. "That's all right, Simon." He turned to Margot who still looked furious. "Naturally I'll replace the suit, Margot."

"That isn't the point, is it?" she snapped. "He is becoming an unpleasant, vicious child and it's time he was taken in hand. Now, I'm going to change."

When she had gone, the three left in the room seemed visibly to relax. Max and Jane looked at each other then at Simon. "Go to your room, Simon," Max said quietly. "I'll come up later."

"But Daddy . . ."

"You heard me. Go on."

Jane made to follow but was called back. "Leave him alone. I don't want you to go making a fuss of him."

She returned to him, her expression troubled. "He's only a little boy."

"He was old enough to know what he was doing when he threw the ink. He's old enough to take the consequences."

"He is only six."

"Are you telling me how to handle my own son, Jane?"

His voice was dangerously low and had Jane not been so upset, she would have heeded the warning and kept silent. As it was, she thought of Simon and that Max was being too hard on him. "No . . . but it seems wrong that he should be punished when he did apologise and . . ."

"Reluctantly and to please you only. Anyway, that is beside the point. The point being, Jane, that you are getting too damn fond of minding my business, and the last thing I need is a little slip of a thing like you interfering in my life. Just remember, you *are* only my secretary, and even that situation can quite easily be altered. Understand me?"

"Yes." She had gone dead white and it took all her will power to stop herself from trembling. If he noticed this, he gave no indication of it.

"Good. Now, just go away, and for God's sake, stop meddling!"

She walked past him, head down, so that he could not see how close to tears she was. Now that she knew she loved him, his fury was unbearable and she simply did not have it in her to face up to him. Her pride seemed to have taken a definite fall, or disappeared altogether and the scarcely veiled threat that he could dismiss her quite easily and without effort, had sent a spasm of pain through her.

Jane ate alone in her room that evening and this time Max did not send for her. She imagined him dining alone with Margot and thought they were probably both glad not to have her there. After dinner there came a soft knock on the door and Simon came in. He wore pyjamas and a red dressing gown and looked pink and flushed, his hair a little damp and neatly combed flat, as though he had just been bathed. He smiled cheerfully at Jane, all signs of the tantrum vanished.

"Are you supposed to be wandering about like that?" Jane inquired, and he nodded, clambering on her bed and sitting cross legged upon it.

"I asked Daddy if I could come and say goodnight and he said I could if I didn't take too long about it and if I said 'I hope I'm not bothering you.'"

"No, you never could bother me," Jane smiled. Far from it, she thought, realising with a pang of dismay that she had been just as foolish over Simon as she had been over Max. She loved the child and knew this could only bring pain in the future. Her life at Mill House was very uncertain and the future by no means assured. She sat on the bed beside Simon.

"I take it you're back in favour again."

"With Daddy. He came up and helped me have my bath and he's going to tell me my goodnight story now. He said I was very naughty to throw the ink but I think he really thought it was funny."

This picture of a domesticated Max warmed Jane. Even if she was out of favour with her unpredictable employer, it was good that he hadn't punished Simon further. "Why did you do it, Simon?"

His little nose wrinkled. "It's her. I hate her. I didn't know she was coming today and then she was talking to Daddy, an' you know we're going to stay with her at Christmas an' I don't want to. We went there before and it was awful. She lives right in the town with no garden and her flat is all smart an' clean and she won't let me have my toys or play or anything. I have to sit still all the time an' not say a word. I hate her."

"But Simon, is that why you threw the ink?"

"No. She told me I wasn't to take Alexander with me. She said I was too big to have him in bed with me."

"Alexander?"

"My Teddy. She said I was a soppy baby and it was time I grew up." His lips trembled and the huge blue eyes filled with tears. Jane touched the thick dark hair gently and thought that given half the chance, she might throw a bottle of ink at Margot Copeland herself.

"Was your Daddy there when she said this?"

He shook his head. "I didn't tell him in case he said she was right. But she wasn't right, was she, Jane? I love Alexander and I couldn't go to sleep without him."

"No, love, she wasn't right. But if she says such things again, it might be better to tell your

Daddy. Going round throwing bottles of ink doesn't solve anything."

"I know." He moved suddenly, wrapping his arms round Jane's neck and holding her tightly, snuffling at her ear in a way that was uniquely his. "I love you, Jane. I wish . . . is my Daddy going to *marry* her?"

Jane's arms tightened spasmodically. "I don't know, Simon."

"I'll run away if he does. I don't want *her* to be my Mummy. I wish you were. Jane, couldn't you marry my Daddy?"

"Oh, Simon!" Jane rubbed her cheek against his dark head then eased him off her shoulder. "We can't always have what we want in life, darling. I'm afraid you'll have to learn that." She kissed his cheek. "Go to bed, dear. Goodnight."

When Simon got back to his bedroom, a bright, lively room that perfectly reflected the personality of the child, a room littered with boyish toys, a fort complete with medieval knights and all set up for a siege, model aeroplanes hanging from the ceiling, posters of tanks, planes and ships all over the walls, he found his father still sitting on the bed flicking through a copy of *Wind in the Willows* which was Simon's current favourite. They smiled at each other with familiarity and fondness and Max asked, "All right?"

"Yes. Jane said I never could bother her."

"Jane is altogether too forbearing," Max said. "Come on, my lad, into bed. It's high time you were asleep."

Simon scrambled into bed and allowed the covers to be pulled up under his chin. Max glanced round and realised something was missing.

"Where's Alexander?"

"In the cupboard," Simon replied, his eyes very wide and alert.

"Oh, dear. Gone off him, have you?"

"No."

Max fetched the battered old Teddy Bear and looked him over, not understanding the significance of the act, or why his son looked suddenly so happy and even relieved. "Can't have Alexander left out in the cold," he said cheerfully.

"No. He was your Teddy, wasn't he, Daddy?"

"He was. Which all goes to show how ancient he is. Come on, son, sleep."

"Can I have a bit of *A and A* first?"

"Oh, lord, must you?" *A and A* was the shortened name of a continuing story of a set of rather revolting twins with the unlikely names of Algernon and Amy, which he had started when Simon was four. It had begun as a simple enough story of these two children going off to search for their father who had been captured by pirates, but had escalated from there, mainly because, as Max could never think of a satisfactory conclusion, he had added to it as he went along. As Simon had never suffered from nightmares or bad dreams in all his young life, Max was in no way restricted by having to leave out anything guaranteed to frighten a more sensitive child.

"Just a bit of it, please," Simon begged.

"All right. Where did we get to?"

"They were in the dungeons and had found the treasure."

"Oh, yes, and there were two skeletons beside the treasure chest. They had been left there to guard the treasure and were armed to the teeth with knives, flint lock pistols, swords and cutlasses—but they had starved to death hundreds of years earlier . . ." The story continued for about ten minutes, while Simon watched his father with steady eyes. *A and A* never sent him to sleep though he always slept well afterwards. Following the time honoured tradition of leaving the audience gasping for more, Max finished on a high note, as the twins, while exploring the deserted castle, heard the sounds of clanking chains coming from the battlements.

"That'll do," he said. "Sleep."

"Okay." Simon snuggled down, looking very angelic. "Daddy . . ."

"Mmmmm?"

"I do love Jane."

"Do you?"

"I wish she could stay with us forever. She could, couldn't she?"

"I don't know about that. I imagine Jane will eventually want to go away and live her own life."

"I bet she likes it with us best of all."

"You do, do you?"

"It would be nice, wouldn't it, Daddy, if you married Jane and then she could be my Mummy and stay here for ever?"

"Oh, God, Simon! Six years old is far too young to start match making." Max sat back on the bed and surveyed his son with mild exasperation. "You have to learn that just because you want something, doesn't mean you can necessarily have it."

"That's what Jane said, more or less."

"You mean you put this . . . er . . . suggestion, to Jane?" Simon nodded, the angelic look increasing as he smiled beatifically. "What did she say?"

"She said—you can't always have what you want in life. Or something like that."

"Very true. Now for heaven's sake, Simon, go to

sleep. And kindly allow me to do my own courting, if and when I want to. Right?"

"Right. Night night, Daddy."

"Goodnight, nuisance." Max kissed him lightly on the forehead, reflecting that for a very young child, Simon managed to create a great many problems, as well as making equally interesting suggestions. He went out and Simon, content in the knowledge that neither party in question had completely scoffed at his idea, went peacefully to sleep, still smiling.

On the morning following the ink incident, the atmosphere at Mill House was still somewhat strained; the only one not at all affected was Simon. His prep school had broken up for the Christmas holidays and he was very much in evidence about the house, getting in everyone's way. Max had reached a difficult part of the book and spent much of the morning staring out of the window or moodily prowling about the room, hands deep in pockets, shoulders hunched. Occasionally he would bark out a sentence or ask Jane to read something back to him, and once, when she misread her shorthand, he knew at once and snapped at her that if she couldn't do better than that, she had better start looking for a new job. Having learned that when he was in this kind of mood it was better to keep quiet, Jane said nothing. Only later in the morning did matters improve. Simon came in, full of himself, amusing them both with his chatter but completely interrupting any flow of the creative spirit. Eventually Max picked his son up and put him outside the door.

"Go away, nuisance. I promise I'll give you my time later. Just go away and find someone else to pester." He turned from the door and met Jane's eyes. His expression lightened then and he smiled. Rather uncertainly, she returned the smile and he sighed heavily and came over to her, sitting near her, elbows on his desk, rubbing his eyes wearily.

"Oh, Jane, I'm sorry I snapped at you. I'm in a foul mood. I realise what a bastard I'm being and I don't seem able to stop myself. The book isn't going well but that's no reason to take it out on you." He smiled apologetically at her. He was the sort of man, Jane thought ruefully, as her blood and bones seemed to melt away, who could half kill someone and then smile disarmingly at them and be forgiven. She saw the little lines of fatigue round his eyes and longed to kiss them away.

"It doesn't matter. Perhaps you need a break."

"Yes. Well, Christmas is nearly here."

"Yes . . ." she hesitated, then murmured, "Simon tells me you're going to stay with Mrs. Copeland at Christmas."

"That's right. It's not a very popular move with him. He and Margot seem to be somewhat at loggerheads at the moment. Strange really as they usually get on very well."

"Do they?" She hadn't intended sounding so sceptical but he threw her a direct, searching glance as she felt her colour rise. "Of course, I know nothing about it."

"Liar," he said softly. "It seems to me you are much more in Simon's confidence than anyone else is. Did he tell you why he threw that ink?"

Jane nodded, but when he looked enquiringly at her, said, "I think perhaps you should ask Simon yourself."

"I see. Still no telling tales, eh? Whatever the reason, it doesn't excuse what he did."

"I don't suppose it does."

"All the same, in a way it was quite funny." Suddenly his lips twitched with amusement and he let out a little chuckle of laughter. "You should have seen her face!"

He didn't sound at all like a man talking about the woman he loved and Jane, warmed by the short moment of intimacy, laughed too. "I wish I had." Her laughter was cut short as she became aware that he was watching her searchingly. She remembered then that only two days before she had stood here in this very room, almost naked in his arms, receiving his kisses and kissing him in return. The colour rushed to her face and she looked away from him, thinking that if he really had forgotten those lovely moments, he would wonder at the blush and its cause.

He patted her hand lightly. "Back to work, Jane. Read me that last paragraph, please."

She went into dinner that evening wearing a straight, simple dress of navy blue, and with her hair gleaming and straight down her back, loosed from its usual chignon. She looked very young and virginal, in marked contrast to the sophisticated, older woman look of Margot. Once during the meal she became aware of Max watching her, his eyes troubled, but she could not tell what he was thinking. Margot was coolly distant and only Simon chattered happily. Jane remembered what she had intended telling him yesterday, and turned to Max.

"Will you and Simon be back here the day after New Year's Day?"

He nodded. "I don't suppose we'll be away more than a week."

"The local dramatic society is doing *Cinder-*

ella at the village hall and I thought, if you didn't mind, that I might take Simon."

Before Max could reply, Simon had cried out excitedly, "Oh, yes, I can go, Daddy, can't I? Say I can, please!"

Max laughed and again opened his mouth to reply. This time he was forestalled by Margot who was looking at Jane with open dislike.

"Really, Miss Murray, the least you could have done is consult Mr. Carstairs first, before making such a ridiculous suggestion. As though Simon could be allowed to mix with the rabble just to watch some amateurs perform in the village hall! If Simon wishes to see a pantomime, I will arrange for him to go to the Palladium while he is in London. Much more suitable."

Jane stared at Margot in blank dismay, at the same time aware that Max was looking in the same direction, though his face was without expression and it was difficult to know what he was thinking. At length he said, "Margot, I really don't think this has anything to do with . . ."

He got no further, for with a yell, Simon leapt off his chair, purple faced with fury and indignation. "I will go with Jane! I will! I hate you! This is nothing to do with you. I don't want to go anywhere with you! I want to go with Jane!"

Max shouted his name, but he spoke to thin air for Simon had rushed out of the room. He stood up, at the same time as Jane also got to her feet, her eyes dark with distress.

"Leave him," Max said.

Jane shook her head slowly. Suddenly it was more important to go to Simon, even at the risk of alienating Max completely. She said, her voice high and clear, touchingly young and proud, "I'm sorry, but I think Simon is right, even though his way of expressing himself is a little violent. There's nothing wrong with him going to the pantomime in the village. And if the people there are rabble . . . well, I am too."

She turned and walked away. If Max wanted to side with Margot, that was his affair. If he did, he wasn't worth her own love or her respect.

In the hall she hesitated, wondering where Simon had gone, and finally went upstairs to his room. This was empty but she noticed the door to her own room was ajar. Simon was in the corner farthest away from the door, crouched down and facing the wall, crying wretchedly and miserably. Any thoughts of recrimination fled from Jane. In seconds he was in her arms, gathered up against her and she held him tightly, almost crying with him.

"Don't, darling, don't cry anymore. It's all right. I promise you it'll be all right. Don't cry, Simon. Come on, love." She sat on the bed, lifting him on to her lap and gently ruffling his hair. He still sobbed, harshly and wordlessly, his little body racked and in agony. Jane felt that she would willingly slap Margot Copeland across her beautifully made-up face.

"I want to go with you, Jane. I want to. I don't want to go with her. And now . . . and now I've made her angry again and she said . . . she said . . ." He hiccoughed loudly and burst into renewed floods of tears. There was more here than was immediately obvious, Jane thought as she mopped him up again.

"What did she say, darling?"

"She said if I was nasty again she would punish me. She said when she was married to Daddy, she'd make him send me to a boarding school and I would have to stay there, even in the holidays, and I'd hardly ever come home or see Daddy. But I don't want to go away!"

Jane moved back and looked at the stricken young face. Could Margot really have said anything so cruel? Could anyone be so callous and unfeeling? She gave Simon a little shake.

"Listen. She won't do that. You won't be sent away, Simon. I know your Daddy won't do that. No matter what she said, he would never do such a thing."

"He would!" he gulped. "She said it!"

"Then she was wrong," a very quiet voice, slightly husky with emotion, said, and Max walked into the room. Jane looked up at him over the head of his son, her love in her eyes for him to see. But he was looking, not at her, but at Simon. She wondered how long he had been there, listening at the partially open door. He was very distressed and grave, and came over to her, taking Simon into his arms. He held the boy hard, saying a little unsteadily, "You aren't going anywhere, Simon, you have no fear of that."

"Really and truly, Daddy?"

"Really and truly." Max put Simon on the bed beside Jane and sat down himself, giving his son a smile. "The only place you're going is to see *Cinderella* with Jane after Christmas." Simon's face magically lit up. It was still smudged with the dirty streaks the tears had caused but he was happy again, as instantly restored as a child can be.

"Really and truly, Daddy?"

"Really and truly," Max repeated obediently and a little self consciously. "If it weren't for the fact that I'll be in America, I would ask Jane to get an extra ticket and go with you." He touched Simon's hair gently. "We don't go out together

117

enough, do we? Maybe in the summer we can find a circus or something of the sort for us to go to."

"Oh . . . Daddy!" Simon breathed, as though this was the most wonderful thing in the world that could happen to him. He looked up into his father's face, awe struck, numbed happiness in the shining, dark blue eyes. Max, his hand still on Simon's hair, had something like wonder on his face. Jane guessed he hadn't realised the extent of Simon's love for him. She smiled at them both and was conscious of a sort of yearning ache, a feeling of being an outsider, not belonging to anyone or anything. Max looked at her then, his mouth relaxing into a sweet, gentle curve.

"Thank you for offering to take him, Jane."

"I'm only too pleased," she murmured formally, and added, uncertainly. "I should have mentioned it to you first."

"Nonsense. You're in no way to blame for this. And now, would you mind putting Simon to bed, please. He looks done in after all this . . . melodrama." His eyes laughed at her, teasing her gently and in the nicest possible way. He stood up, after kissing Simon lightly on the forehead. "I have something that must be done," he said meaningfully, and left them to return to Margot.

As Jane helped Simon have his bath and bundled him into bed, she reflected that she would dearly love to be a fly on the wall at that moment!

Six

Any notions Jane might have had about Margot being sent packing were soon shattered. The next day, a Saturday, she was still very much in evidence in Mill House, as coolly confident and complacent as ever. Perhaps, Jane thought sadly, she and Max really were so close that he needed only to put her straight about Simon and from then on nothing would be said. Probably Max only lost his temper with stupid little secretaries that had no more sense than to go falling helplessly and hopelessly in love with him!

It had snowed again overnight, covering the snow that had been there a week now with fresh whiteness and, looking out of her window that overlooked the lawns, Jane saw Max and Simon going out to where Simon's snowman stood. They were holding hands, Simon giving an occasional little skip as though to show how happy he was. The sensation of being on the outside looking in was very strong in Jane as she watched them, glad that there was this love between them but regretful that she had no part in it. Sighing, she turned from the window and her eyes fell upon her camera, that lay upon the bedside table. It was a perfect day for taking photographs, a crisp, cold, blue-skied day, and she knew that when she left Mill House it would be a small comfort to have some snaps to remind her of these bitter-sweet days. She pulled on some warm clothing and went outside, crossing the lawn to where Max was helping Simon put some more snow on the much depleted snowman. Seeing her, Simon came skipping and hopping towards her.

She showed the camera to Max. "I wondered if I might take some photos of Simon," she said rather diffidently. "It's just the right kind of day." She was hesitant, thinking that he might object, but he merely smiled and told her to go ahead.

Simon was delighted at the prospect of being photographed. He strutted about proudly, posing in a natural way, somehow instinctively falling into the right positions so that Jane began to suspect he must have inherited Max's acting ability along with his looks, and even Max drawled, "You ought to be on the stage, my lad."

Jane took several shots of Simon playing in the snow and he insisted on having one taken with his snowman. Then Simon reached for his father, pulling him eagerly towards the snowman, and Jane obligingly snapped them both. It would, she thought even as she clicked the shutter, be something to keep, her own private picture of them both.

Max came over to her then and took the camera from her. "I'll take one of you and Simon," he said, "and no doubt the inevitable snowman."

"I've never had a really truly snowman before," Simon explained, "And I want a picture to show the boys at school." He grinned toothily at the camera as Max aimed at them, then said, "Can I take one now?"

"You?" Jane laughed. "I don't think you'd be able to manage the camera, love."

"I could. I bet I could. Couldn't I, Daddy?"

"Couldn't you what?" Max asked, joining them. "Take a photo? I doubt it."

But Simon looked so woebegone that Jane relented. It was the most simple form of Instamatic camera and if he messed up the picture it would mean the loss of only one frame. She explained to him what to do. "Don't press the shutter until you see exactly what you want in there—see? And keep your fingers away from the lens."

He nodded. "I can do it. I bet I can. I bet it'll be the best one of all. You go and stand by the snowman—and you, Daddy."

"This will be a lovely picture of our feet," Max murmured with a grin. He draped himself against the snowman, putting one arm round its broad shoulders and contriving to look, even in that ridiculous pose, dramatically handsome. "This okay, Simon?" he called, and they all laughed.

"That's super, Daddy," Simon shouted excitedly. "I can see you in here. Quick, Jane, before I go all wobbly."

Jane obediently stood on the other side of the snowman from Max. "Is this all right?"

"No. I can't see you. Only half of you anyway."

"Come round here, Jane," Max said lazily. "Simon, you can do without the snowman for once. If you want to cut anyone in half, make it him." He took Jane's wrist, encircling it with long, hard fingers, propelling her to stand beside him and, as she stood there, uncertain, wanting to move away yet at the same time wanting his closeness, he drew her to his side, his right arm hard across her shoulders. She knew how stiff she was, terrified of the tumult of emotions that flashed through her, and he said, looking at Simon still, "Relax, Jane, you're only having your photograph taken, not having a tooth pulled. Okay, Simon?" He looked down at Jane then and she, rather shyly, raised her eyes to his, reading unknown but somehow delightful thoughts in his smile and feeling his arm tighten, drawing her closer still to him. Then, as Jane felt as though she was drowning in his dark blue eyes, Simon clicked the camera shutter.

"You weren't looking at me," he said accusingly. "I said watch the birdie."

Almost reluctantly, Max removed his arm from Jane's shoulder, smiling enigmatically at her; Jane looked away from him, dazed by what she thought she had seen in his eyes. Only then did she notice that Margot had come out of the house and was by the porch watching them. It was obvious from the taut look round her mouth that she had been witness to the brief intimate moment between Jane and Max. Jane took the camera from Simon, willing her hands not to shake. "I'll take the film to the village to be developed. Simon, why don't we go and use up the last few frames now? I'll take a few of the house." She took his hand, glancing uncertainly at Max, but he was already walking towards Margot. Jane heard him call, "Hello, Margot. Are you off?"

"I thought I would stay until tomorrow if you don't mind."

"Of course I don't. You know you're always welcome to stay for as long as you wish." They went into the house, Margot's arm through his, and Jane looked quickly away, summoned by Simon's urgent tug on her hand.

* * *

After lunch Max drove into Southampton, taking Simon with him. Before leaving, he asked Jane if she would do some extra typing for him so she went along to the library where she was rather disconcerted to discover Margot sitting before the fire. Jane hesitated in the doorway, then walked in, not at all eager to get drawn into a conversation; what Margot had said to Simon still rankled bitterly. "Is there anything I can do for you, Mrs. Copeland?" she inquired, taking refuge in her best secretarial manner.

"No, though I rather think there is something I can do for you."

"Oh?" Jane sat at her desk and fiddled uneasily with some papers. "I can't imagine what you can do for me."

"I can save you a lot of trouble and heartache."

Jane looked up sharply, watching as Margot sat down again, reclining elegantly in the big leather armchair that Max used. She crossed one leg over the other and took her time lighting a Gauloise cigarette.

"Perhaps you could explain what you mean, Mrs. Copeland," Jane suggested quietly. "I wasn't aware that I was heading for trouble or heartache."

"If you go on as you are doing, you will certainly have both. I will be honest with you, Miss Murray, though the truth may be painful. When I first saw you I thought you would do well enough as Mr. Carstairs' secretary. You are rather young but your qualifications are good and you seemed reasonably level headed. Certainly sensible enough not to get ideas about your employer."

"Ideas?" Jane interrupted. "I don't . . ."

"Let me finish please. I suppose I underestimated Max's attractions. He is, of course, a

123

devastatingly attractive man, and his life, his talent, add to that attraction. However, I thought he would in no way encourage you. You are not the sort of female to appeal to a man like Max. You are young and look younger, you are in no way beautiful, in fact I would say you are completely without desire. I don't suppose Max has done anything to give you the impression that he finds you attractive. If he has, I can assure you it is purely through habit. He is one of those men who can't resist making every woman in sight fall in love with them."

She paused a moment and the silence was broken by a sudden loud cracking noise. Both women looked at Jane's hands. She had been holding a pencil and now stared blankly at the two pieces.

"You are a sensible girl, Miss Murray. I suggest you pack your cases and leave at once. I can find a temporary secretary for Mr. Carstairs. Naturally I shall see that you are not the loser financially."

"You mean you intend paying me off?" Jane's voice didn't sound like her own. In an effort to stop it shaking, she hardened it so that every word sounded stilted and peculiar. The strange thing was, she wasn't upset. She was just angry, very, very angry. The violence of the emotion that flooded through her caused her to tremble and her heart pounded as though it would burst. She said, very softly, "I'm beginning to understand why Simon threw that ink at you. Had I a bottle handy, I might just do the same thing!"

Margot got to her feet, magnificent in her affronted anger. "How dare you!"

"I dare very well. How *you* dare is what amazes me."

"I shall tell Max what a rude, ungrateful girl you

are. You can be sure he will dismiss you on the spot."

"You do that, Mrs. Copeland," Jane snapped. "Tell him everything, all about what sort of man you seem to think he is. I'm sure he'll be interested to know that you think him some kind of Casanova. You just tell him everything."

"I am not staying a moment longer to listen to such nonsense. You just think about my words, girl, and get out before you are thrown out."

When she had gone, Jane breathed a sigh of relief and smiled faintly, rather pleased with herself. She still did not know what the relationship was between Max and Margot, but she was fairly certain Margot would not mention the conversation to him.

Christmas day was on a Friday that year and Max and Simon were due to drive up to London on Christmas Eve. Jane took Simon into the village on Wednesday to fetch the photographs she had taken. Simon asked if he could stay outside, while she went into the chemist shop.

"All right. But don't wander off anywhere."

As she waited for her change, Jane took a quick glance through the photos. On the whole they were very good particularly the one she had taken of Max and Simon together. She smiled to herself when she looked at the snap Simon had taken. She and Max were both in it, though the snowman was more in evidence than it should have been, and they all leaned precipitously to the left. Max and she were looking at each other, amazingly lover-like, and Jane remembered the delightful sensation that had gone through her as he held her against him. Her smile was soft and reflective as she went outside to find Simon. He was looking up at a tall man who wore a sheepskin jacket. Jane halted in the shop doorway, a startled cry escaping her lips as her eyes met Alistair's. He smiled as he saw her and came over, taking her hand in a hearty handshake.

"Jane, my dear, what a surprise," he said affably. "I thought I recognised you as you went into the shop. This young fellow tells me he's Max Carstairs' son."

"That's right." Jane handed Simon the photographs and moved away a little so that Simon could not hear. "Alistair, what are you doing here?"

"Just seeing how the land lies, sweetie. Don't get upset. The boy thinks our meeting is pure coincidence. I thought you'd have got in touch with me before now."

"I . . . I've been busy. I have to do a proper job of work, you know, and you told me to settle in."

"Of course, but it's been . . . what? Seven, eight weeks."

Simon interrupted them, coming over with a skip of delight. "I told you I could do it, Jane. See, I got you and Daddy in. An' these others are good too."

"Can I see?" Before Jane could prevent him, Alistair had taken the photographs and was looking interestedly through them. He glanced shrewdly at Jane, his smile broadening. "Very good," he said to Simon, and then, "I beg your pardon, Jane, obviously you have been busy."

"No!" she gasped, almost snatching the pictures from him. "It isn't like that. I only . . ."

"It's all right, my dear, don't bother to explain." He smiled again and looked very pleased with himself and her. "I'll be hearing from you—after Christmas perhaps. Will you be staying here?"

"Yes."

"I see. Well, goodbye for now. Goodbye Simon."

Simon said "Goodbye," cheerfully dismissing him, probably forgetting him the moment he got into his car. Jane could not forget so easily. She was disturbed by a restlessness, a worry, that nagged at her mind, not just during the walk home but all that day and the following days. Why hadn't she told Alistair outright that she couldn't do the job she had set out to do? That the photographs were for her own pleasure and not for use in his magazine? Even later, while she and Max laughed over the snaps and he asked her to get copies of them all for him, she was miserable so that he asked if she was feeling all right.

"Yes. I'm fine, thanks."

"You look a bit low. I suppose it's with Christmas coming up and you being stuck here. Look, Jane, are you sure you want to stay? I know I said I would find you some work, but I was in a bad mood at the time and never meant it, of course. I can't see you having a very gay time."

She smiled quickly, grateful for his concern and for the apology that lurked beneath his words. "My Christmases have never been very gay affairs, and at least here the surroundings will be lovely."

On the morning he left Mill House for London, Jane handed Max a parcel. "This is for Simon. I wonder if you would mind giving it to him on Christmas morning, please."

"Of course. Thank you, Jane. And as we are

swapping presents, this is for you, not to be opened till Christmas day, from Simon . . . and from me." She took the small, gaily wrapped parcel with murmured thanks and a blush of pleasure. Then, before she could think, certainly before she had time to enjoy it, he had leaned forward and kissed her softly on the cheek.

"Happy Christmas, Jane," he said and walked out to his car. Jane followed more slowly, her brain pounding with confused delight. She waved to Simon, who was still protesting that he didn't want to go, then she returned to the house, one hand resting against her cheek in blissful remembrance.

Seven

It was Boxing Day and Jane was alone at Mill House as the rest of the staff had gone down to the village to watch the traditional meeting of the local hunt. Depressed and restless, Jane fetched her coat and went out. It was a beautiful day; the snow had melted some days before but there had been a frost overnight and it was very cold though the sky was summer blue. The frozen grass crackled beneath her booted feet as she walked across the lawns, surrounded by misty clouds of her own breath. She paused by the rose garden and on impulse pushed open the low, wrought iron gate and went inside. The design of the garden was unusual and attractive; a crazy path spiralled into the centre where there was an ornate Victorian sundial. Jane walked the long way round the spiral and bent to look at the sundial. The circular copper dial was covered in moss and grime, completely indistinguishable. Like everything else here, it was dying of neglect. Jane straightened up and looked round her, only then noticing another gate on the far side of the garden from the one by which she had entered. It was a tall gate and locked. Through it she saw trees and long, unkempt grass, nothing to entail a lock. She rattled the gate but it wouldn't budge so she left it and returned the way she had come. She had reached the small gate when she halted, a look of incredulous joy flooding across her face, as she saw Max walking towards her. He raised one hand in a normal gesture and smiled cheerfully, no doubt unaware that his sudden and unexpected appearance had sent her blood soaring, her knees trembling. He was wearing dark grey slacks and a thick, warm looking cashmere sweater over an open neck shirt.

"I didn't . . . I didn't expect you," she murmured shyly.

"I don't suppose you did. I came back because there was something I had to do." The statement was cryptic but she was too stunned and happy to think of questioning him about it.

"Is Simon with you?"

"No."

There was silence while they looked at each other, then she half turned away, frightened yet happy, afraid of showing him that his appearance had put her instantly in heaven. "I was looking at the rose garden," she said a little breathlessly. He looked past her into the garden. "It should be looked after," she said softly. "It would be so pretty if it was tidied up."

"I've neglected everything," he said sadly. "Diane used to see to all this." It was the first time he had ever mentioned Simon's mother to Jane, but he sounded without real regret. He looked at her, his eyes unreadable, and smiled faintly. The silence this time was uncomfortable though he didn't seem to mind. He stood before her, hands deep in trouser pockets, looking at her. She searched desperately for something to say. "There's a gate over there. It's locked."

"Yes. It leads to . . . did it intrigue you, Jane? What would you expect to find beyond it? Something secret and magical?"

"You're laughing at me," she said a little reproachfully.

"No, I'm not. Not unkindly anyway. I've been unkind enough to you in the past, Jane, and have no cause to be so about your imagination."

She looked up sharply, surprised by the fervour in his voice. "Why is it locked then?"

He led the way to the gate and proceeded to search about in the undergrowth until he came across a tin from which he took a key. He grinned at Jane's surprised face and explained, "This is Simon's favourite place in the summer and all this cloak and dagger stuff is his idea." He swung open the gate and let her walk past him. On the other side was a small copse, very overgrown and almost impenetrable in parts. Max took Jane's arm at the elbow, his hand, even through her jacket, feeling warm and possessively exciting.

"Here we are," he said as they rounded the little copse, and Jane gave a gasp of delight. At their feet the ground sloped away in a series of small, grass-covered terraces leading down to a flat, stage-like area. It was a perfect, circular amphitheatre, not completely natural as Jane had at first thought, though the designer had cleverly used the natural contours of the land in forming the circular stage and the rows and rows of terraces that surrounded it.

"It was built when Mill House was a school," Max explained. "They used to hold regular seasons here, every summer, Shakespeare generally, but also Greek tragedy."

"Didn't you . . . ?" Jane began to ask, then

hastily held her tongue, imagining she had wandered over the line he had drawn between her and his private life. He looked enquiringly down at her, his mien so relaxed and amiable that she dared to continue. "I think Philip mentioned that you went to this school."

He nodded and walked on, so that she rushed to keep up with his long strides. "This was built already, at that time." He stopped walking and looked down at the stage. "I had my first taste of acting on this stage," he said and his smile was softly reminiscent.

"Which part?"

He laughed then. "It was a boy's school and our drama master had no aversion to dressing boys up for female parts, as of course happened in Shakespeare's time. Believe it or not, I was Ophelia!"

Jane threw back her head and laughed unaffectedly. "Oh, Max, no!" She blushed at her careless use of his name, lowered her head and murmured, "I'm sorry."

"For what? I did suggest we dispense with the formality of 'Mr. Carstairs,' didn't I?"

As this short statement made it abundantly obvious that he had not forgotten that night in the library at all, Jane was grateful that he walked on as he spoke. Wave after wave of embarrassment revealed itself in the heightened colour of her face and she plodded after him, her head lowered, brought up short when he stopped walking and she collided with him.

"Sorry," she murmured, keeping her head averted and thus missing the tender amusement that flickered over his face. She looked down at the amphitheatre. "Do the acoustics work?"

"I imagine so. Why don't you test them?"

"How?"

"Go down and say something. I'll tell you if I can hear."

"What should I say?"

He shrugged. "Anything. I can't imagine a woman being completely lost for words. Recite a poem or something."

She walked away, treading down the steep steps that had been cut into the soil. As she walked on to the stage she felt the thrill of knowing that it was here that Max had taken that first step upon a road to a career that had made him world famous, a career that had, moreover, ended here also. Why had he given up the stage, she wondered? Not, as had been suggested, because of the accident, or the scar on his face. She was sure that despite the slight bitterness he had displayed when she first saw it, he was not bothered at all by the scar. No, whatever his reasons, the disfigurement had nothing to do with it.

"Come on!" he called out impatiently and she plunged into *She Walks in Beauty*, the only thing she could think of on the spur of the moment. When she had finished and walked back up the slope towards him, he made no immediate comment on her recitation but only on her choice.

"I didn't imagine you would be a fan of Byron."

"Why? A very romantic character was Byron. I fell for him when I was thirteen or so and had a large print of that portrait of him by Phillips on my bedroom wall." A print, she remembered that had been accompanied by pictures of Max himself, as well as the Beatles and Rolling Stones. Her taste in those days had been diverse to the extreme. She wondered, with amusement, what Max would think if she told him this.

"Anyway," he was saying, "the acoustics obviously do work. You were mumbling something awful but I could hear you."

"Mumbling? I was not!" she cried indignantly, at the same time gathering together her wits and her nerve to say what she knew she had intended saying from the first moment of seeing this wonderful place. She realised that this was, somehow, a very important moment, certainly for her and perhaps even for him.

"Show me how it's done," she suggested softly.

"What?"

"It's your turn now."

He looked straight at her for a very long moment, a moment in which she returned his gaze unblinkingly, determined not to give way and lower her eyes. Then he nodded very slightly, an almost royal gesture that revealed the actor in him, and walked away from her, down the grassy slope to the stage. Once there he turned and looked up at her, running one hand over his hair before thrusting both hands into trouser pockets.

"What's it to be?" he asked, his voice soft but carrying easily to her ears.

"Henry V," she replied without thought.

"'Once more into the breach' I suppose," he suggested, his voice slower now and with more of its usual drawl.

"No. St. Crispin's Day. 'Gentlemen of England now a-bed.'"

He inclined his head. "Discerning girl. Very well."

There was silence then for what might have been at least a minute, a silence broken by Jane's uneven breathing and the sudden shrill song of a blackbird in the beech tree above her head. She was a girl again, ten years old and wearing her first long dress. Her father was beside her, alive and gay, and she sat there, a thin, tense young girl, still gawky and clumsy with youth, idolising the slim, handsome young actor on the stage.

The fourteen-years-older Max was standing very still, shoulders hunched, as though deep in thought. Then he raised his head, looking in the direction of his solitary audience but not seeing her, and then the words came to her, flowing over her with a breath-catching beauty that left her without thought or mind for anything but his voice and the words he spoke.

"'This day is call'd the feast of Crispian.
He that outlives this day, and comes safe home
Will stand a tip-toe when this day is nam'd,
And rouse him at the name of Crispian . . .'"

The speech continued, coming easily now, not rusty or stilted as from disuse, but as though he had spoken it every day of his life. In her mind Jane saw the king, armour gleaming in the sunlight of France, and above him the host of flags and pennons fluttering in the breeze; the leopards of England, gold on red, and fleur de lys, silver on blue. She did not know that she was holding her breath, or that her hands were clenched into fists, or that tears were streaming down her face.

. . ."'And gentlemen of England now a-bed
Shall think themselves accursed they were not here.
And hold their manhoods cheap while any speaks
That fought with us upon St. Crispin's Day.'"

His voice died away and Jane blinked, and

suddenly there was no young king, glittering with valour and ambition and courage, but a man in twentieth-century clothing, grey slacks and dark cashmere sweater. She caught her lower lip between her teeth to prevent it trembling and watched him stride easily up the slope towards her. He saw the tears and stopped dead a few feet from her, obviously surprised.

"What is it, Jane? That speech is supposed to inflame the blood, to make you want to sing *Rule Brittania* and wave the Union Jack. It isn't supposed to bring on tears." He smiled, very tenderly and came close to her, rubbing a large tear away from her cheek with feather-light finger tips. "Why the tears, Jane?"

She sniffed inelegantly. "I don't know. It reminded me of so much—my father took me to see you in *Henry V* at Stratford when I was ten. I've never forgotten it. I'm sorry. I'm being silly."

"No," he said softly. "Not silly, Jane. You might be a lot of things—stiff-necked, touchy, a bit naïve and very kind and sweet—but never silly." His hand moved to the back of her head, drawing her closer, and he leaned forward, kissing her gently on the mouth. Her lips responded tremulously as she closed her eyes and he kissed her wet face, tasting the salt tears and licking them off in a gesture at once sensual and unutterably loving.

"Stop crying, you funny little thing!" he murmured, laughing softly as he found her mouth again with his. This time the kiss went on longer, and in a moment his arms went round her, pulling her close to him. He felt warm and comfortable in the thick sweater and there was a tenderness about his kiss that had been absent on the other two occasions they had kissed. He moved back and smiled at her, and when she returned the smile, they kissed again, for a long, long time, until Jane's brain whirled with the wonder of it. She returned the kisses with eagerness, loving him so much that in the end the words were torn from her. "Oh, Max, I do love you!"

He stared at her as though the confession surprised him, and then shook his head slowly, wonderingly, and drew her back into his arms, burying his face against her neck and her loose, sweet-smelling hair. His arms were hard round her and his body had stiffened. She heard him mutter, "No! No, Jane, this is ridiculous." Abruptly he pulled her arms from round his neck and held her away from him, his fingers digging into her upper arms as he shook her, though not ungently. "You mustn't, Jane. There's no future for you in me."

"I'm not looking for a future, Max. I just said I love you, that's all. And I do, really. But I'm not asking anything of you." She smiled lovingly at him and he groaned and pulled her back into his arms, kissing her with a desperation she failed to understand. "I ought to send you away," he muttered into her neck. "You're far too young and sweet to be burdened with me. Don't laugh, Jane. I'm serious. You have a whole lifetime ahead of you, whilst I . . ."

Jane smiled at him and tightened her arms about him. "You're making yourself out to be some kind of Methuselah. Really, Max, you're only fifteen or so years older than me."

"I know. But those years hold a whole lifetime of different experiences. I've already had one career and finished with it, and now I'm well into another." He ran his hands wonderingly over her face. "I haven't led a very good life over the last few years, Jane."

"I don't care about any of that. It doesn't matter. Nothing matters except that I love you. Really and truly, as Simon would say." She moved forward, sliding her arms round his neck, standing on tip-toe in order to reach up and rest her lips against the scar on his face, something she had longed to do for weeks now. He turned his head, kissing her and saying, with a tremble in his voice, "Would you take a chance on me then, Jane?"

She wasn't sure what he meant, but it didn't matter. She nodded. "Anytime, if you want me."

"If I want you." It was his turn to smile. "Yes, Jane, I want you. I've wanted you . . . oh, for a very long time. Certainly before that night in the library."

"I thought you had forgotten that."

"How could I? I know you thought I was stoned but I hadn't had that much to drink. I was sitting there hating myself for what I had said to you at dinner that night and I probably would have got myself plastered if you hadn't turned up. I pretended to forget what happened to save you embarrassment, and because it was as well that you didn't know I really wanted you."

"Why did you . . ." she coloured a little. "If you wanted me, why did you send me away?"

"Oh, because you looked so very young. I've done a lot of things in my life, but I've never gone in for corrupting little girls like you. I knew that another few minutes and I wouldn't have been able to control myself. Then we'd both have regretted it."

"I wouldn't have," she insisted promptly and he let out a shout of laughter. "Brazen hussy," he said, holding her close to him, his arms no longer hard but tender and caring. "Oh, Jane, you make me feel young, just being with you. We'll get married as soon as possible."

"Married?" She stiffened in surprise and he looked down, his eyes alight with amusement.

"What else?"

"I don't know. I didn't think you would want to marry me."

"Jane!" he said sternly. "What are you thinking of? I asked you if you would take a chance on me. What I meant was, are you really sure you're willing to put up with me and my foul moods for the rest of your life?"

She smiled. "Will you be bad tempered and shout and revile me for no reason?" she asked, her eyes twinkling.

"Probably." His mouth twisted ruefully. "And you'll do what you always do, sit there with your eyes lowered demurely until I realise what an unmitigated bastard I am being and long with all my heart to take you in my arms and kiss you until you say you forgive me. Only now I really will do that." He took one of her hands and opened it, kissing the palm gently. "I love you, Jane. You've made a man out of the bad-tempered bear I was becoming, and a nice, ordinary child out of the spoilt little monster that Simon was. I don't somehow feel you'll be getting a very good deal, but I'll do what I can to make you happy. If you really can put up with me."

"Oh, yes, Max, I'll put up with you." Her eyes laughed merrily as she daringly added, "I daresay I can think up a few little ways of getting you out of a bad temper."

They strolled back to the gate which Max locked behind them, then through the rose garden, walking round the spiralling path to the sundial in the centre. For a while nothing was said. Jane was too filled with happiness to need to speak. She even felt a little sick, which she supposed was the result of having her wildest dreams and wishes suddenly granted in full. She watched Max's profile as he bent over the sundial trying to decipher the words and symbols upon it, and wondered whether, if she blinked, or pinched herself, she would wake up in bed and discover it was all a dream. Impulsively she put out one hand, resting it on his arm, and he looked inquiringly at her.

"I was just making sure you're really here," she explained simply, and he took her into his arms, proceeding to prove to her with extreme thoroughness that they were both very much there.

"Will you tell Mrs. Copeland?" Jane asked as they walked towards the house.

"I suppose so. I'll have to go and fetch Simon tomorrow."

"She doesn't like me. She . . . she tried to warn me off you," Jane told him frankly.

"Did she now? I'm very glad you took no notice."

"Mrs. Hoskyns told me you were going to marry her."

Max looked amused. "That will teach you not to go listening to gossip. What gave Mrs. H. that idea?"

"She saw you kissing in the library," Jane admitted, rather shame faced, and he laughed again.

"My darling, I'm afraid I've been rather indiscriminate with my kisses in the past. I promise I'll be a good deal more choosey in the future!"

* * *

"You're a very unusual woman, Jane," Max said later. They had eaten dinner together and afterwards went into the library, which was, for both of them, their favourite room. He had built up the fire till it blazed fiercely, turned the lights down to a warm, intimate glow, and taken Jane on to his lap where she curled up contentedly, arms round his neck. She put up one hand and ran her fingers softly over his mouth so that he smiled and bit the fingers lightly.

"Why am I unusual?"

"You seem to lack a woman's greatest vice, curiosity. I thought by now you would be full of questions."

"I am, but I wouldn't ask them. It seems to me that your life is one big question mark, but the past doesn't matter that much."

"Darling, I'm not in the least bothered about talking to you about the past," he smiled tenderly at her. "It suddenly seems very unimportant. What do you want to know, or shall I guess?"

"Can you?"

"You want to know about Diane. A woman always wants to find out about other women who have been in a man's life. Right?"

"I suppose so."

"Diane was like Philip. Which is why I was angry when I thought you and he were getting friendly. I was jealous too, of course, but mainly concerned for you, because Philip is really very shallow, as Diane was, unable to give real affection. I loved Diane when I married her but you can't go on pouring love into an empty shell, getting nothing back. By the time she was killed, we had been separated some months. Having Simon was the final straw for her and she was quite willing for me to have custody of him."

Jane's expression was melancholic; it was terrible to think of the warm, generous man that he must have been, wasting so much love on someone who could not, was unable to return it. Max kissed her full, soft lips. "Don't look so sad. It was all over a long time ago, though not, I suppose, without bitterness. She rather soured me towards your sex, Jane. For a long time I saw women as creatures to be used but definitely not loved. Which is why I treated you so badly; I realised quite soon after you came that I could love you and that, believe me, was the last thing I wanted." He smiled again. "What a fool I was. What a lot of time I wasted fighting against the inevitable."

Jane returned the smile a little shyly and gently rubbed her hand down his face, feeling the roughened skin of the scar. "Why didn't you have this removed after the accident? It could be, couldn't it? Plastic surgery or something?"

He nodded. "Does it bother you?"

"Of course not. It gives you rather a—piratical look. You should have an eye shield to go with it!" She laughed and rubbed her cheek against his. "I just wondered why you hadn't had it removed."

"Soon after the accident I was told I could have it done as soon as the scar had settled—something to do with the scar tissue. I was feeling pretty down about the accident, being the only one, apart from Simon, to come out of it alive, and I certainly wasn't bothered about how I looked. So for a long time I never thought about having anything done. By the time I thought I might, I was already writing with fair success and I was reluctant to waste time going in for the operation. I don't meet that many people and I've been used, for years, to people staring at me, even if for a different reason."

"So it wasn't the accident that made you give up the stage?"

"Lord, no! Nothing so dramatic. The truth, Jane, is very mundane. I simply decided to leave the stage because the pressure was getting too uncomfortable, because I wanted to give my time to Simon—he had no mother and I couldn't leave him for ninety per cent of his life with no father either. And because, for some time I hadn't enjoyed my life. It had suddenly occurred to me that not only was I acting the lives of other people on the stage, I was not even being myself off it. I hardly think I even knew who I really was—when I was acting, when I was being me." He looked seriously at Jane. "That's all, I'm afraid. Is it an anti-climax?"

"No. I'm glad that's all it was. I hated the thought of you being driven from something you loved doing through some inner bitterness and unhappiness."

He leaned his dark head back against the wing of the chair and Jane looked with love at the strong, determined planes of his face. It was still unbelieveable that she was here, close and warm, cradled in his arms as though she had belonged there always. Amazing that only a short while ago she had been plain Miss Murray working for Emerson, Emerson and Marks. That if Alistair hadn't thought of her she . . . she started in a spasm of dismay that brought Max's attention to her.

"What's the matter, my love?"

"Nothing—nothing," she whispered, her eyes huge and dark in the firelight. He studied her face thoughtfully, smiling gently and having no idea of the distress that was coursing through her. He kissed her lightly and she moved in his arms, clinging to him, burying her face in his neck and trying to erase the picture her mind had conjured up. What was the matter with her? How could she have forgotten about Alistair? Or that she was here at Mill House to spy on this man that she loved so much. "I love you!" she whispered urgently, a shudder of apprehension going through her. "Oh, Max, I love you so much!" At her words he bent his head, pressing his mouth on hers, his kisses soon hardening. A moment later the shrill tones of the telephone interrupted them. Max lifted Jane reluctantly off his lap, bestowed a light kiss upon her head and went out into the hall to answer it. Jane knelt on the fur rug by the fire and gazed into the flames. First thing tomorrow she must phone Alistair and tell him she couldn't do the job. Of course she wouldn't mention the relationship between herself and Max. She would just say that she found the idea of the job distasteful. Alistair wasn't unreasonable. He would surely understand.

When Max returned, she felt better and smiled happily at him. "That was Margot," he told her and laughed at the apprehension that slid across Jane's expressive face.

"What did she say? Did you tell her?"

"I did. She was—surprised."

"Surprised? Not angry?"

"Why should she be? Whatever was between us was over a long time ago and I'm sure she is aware of it."

Jane knew better. It was obvious that Max was showing mere masculine denseness about the situation and she was sure Mrs. Copeland would be very, very angry. But then Max reached for her and once in his arms, his mouth ardent and demanding on hers, she could waste no more thoughts on Margot.

Alistair came to the phone within seconds of his secretary reporting that Jane was on the line. Max had gone to fetch Simon and Jane went to the village where she could make the phone call privately. Now, supplied with a handful of ten-penny pieces, she prepared to make her excuses.

"Well, Jane, it's nice to hear from you. I thought you might have phoned before—after seeing me in the village."

"No, I . . . what were you doing there, Alistair?" Jane asked, curiously.

"Just spying out the land. I went up the house and managed to get a few pictures of it, using my tele-foto lens."

Jane was appalled at what she heard. The thought of him creeping about the grounds of Mill House like some kind of James Bond . . . "Anyway, sweetie," he continued, "all I need now are a few words of interest from you and we can go to print. And, of course, those snaps you took of Carstairs and the kid in the snow. They'll go down really well. I didn't have time to look at them properly. Is Carstairs badly disfigured?"

"No!" Jane cried. She felt sick, horrified that she could ever have agreed to do such a filthy job, even to escape Isabel and Malcolm. She must have been out of her mind! "Please listen, Alistair," she pleaded. "I . . . I can't do it. I just can't. I'm sorry, but since I've been here, well, I've realised how awful it would be. I just can't!"

"Now just you cool it, sweetie," he said quite reasonably. "Got cold feet, have you? Look, it won't come back on you. By the time the mag comes to press you'll have left there. You won't be open to Carstairs' wrath and he wouldn't think of creating a ruckus about the article because that would make even more publicity. Don't you worry about it."

"No, Alistair. I can't do it!" she cried desperately.

There was a long pause followed by his heavy, exasperated breathing, then he spoke and his voice, even over the phone, trembled with fury. "You can't do this to me, Jane. I'm relying on this article. The girl at the employment agency was paying back a favour by giving you the job and she won't do it again. I've no hope of getting anyone else in there. Christ, girl, you've got a nerve, springing this on me!"

"I'm sorry," she gulped unhappily.

"Like hell you are. You'd better come up with the goods, Jane, or you really will be sorry. I'll give you one week!" The sound of the receiver being slammed down at the other end of the line echoed in Jane's ears long after she had returned to Mill House.

There was no hope, Max told Jane, of him getting out of the trip to the United States. It had been planned for months and too many people would be disappointed if it was postponed. He left to drive up to Heathrow on the Tuesday following Christmas Day and Jane took Simon out to the car to see him off. They had said their private farewells the previous evening and now, having kissed Simon, telling him to "be good to Jane," Max contented himself with giving her hand a squeeze, mindful of the staff gathered at the front door. They had decided to say nothing to anyone about their getting married.

"We'll get married when I get back and let them all know when it's done," Max said to Jane. "That way there won't be any fuss." Above all he didn't want any fuss. Jane had come to realise that though he was not in the least bothered about meeting people—the lecture tour of the USA proved that—he was still publicity shy and protected his private life which especially included Simon, with the ferocity of a tiger. It was as though he had had so much of being plastered over newspapers and television newsreels when he was on the stage, that he was glad to escape into anonymity now. The lecture tour was a step back into the limelight but Jane knew that the publicity was being very strictly handled and there would be no sensationalism. Of course, Michael Collins, the writer, hadn't the same appeal as Max Carstairs, the actor, but Jane guessed how horrified Max would be at the thought of being splashed all over the glossy pages of *Looking Glass*.

Max got into the Mercedes and drove away with a cheerful wave, and then Jane took Simon back inside. She had a fortnight with nothing to do except look after Simon. Last night Max had said, "I wish this trip had been arranged for some other time. We didn't spend Christmas together but we could at least have seen the New Year in together."

"There will be other Christmases and New Years," Jane reassured him.

"A whole life time of them, my lovely Jane," he had murmured, taking her into his arms.

The highlight of the fortnight was, of course, the pantomime. It was an amateurish performance that would, Jane suspected, have confirmed all Margot Copeland's worst suspicions, with lines forgotten or fluffed and the scenery occasionally swaying dangerously. But all the traditional elements of the pantomime were present and plenty of audience participation. Simon threw himself with enthusiasm into it, his flushed, glowing face all Jane needed to see to know that the pantomime was a success. She had been slightly on edge, mindful of Alistair's threat that she had a week to send her article to him. The week was gone with no sign of anything drastic happening so she could now relax, assured that his threats were idle ones. She was able to enjoy the pantomime herself, regretful only that Max was not sitting beside her, imagining how they would laugh together.

"It was the most loveliest thing I ever saw," Simon murmured when he snuggled down into bed after his supper and bath. "Daddy used to be an actor you know, Jane."

"I know, dear."

"Did he do things like *Cinderella*, do you think?"

Jane bit back her laughter at the thought. "No, love. I rather think your Daddy was in more serious things."

Simon giggled. "I can't really imagine Daddy in *Cinderella*."

"Neither can I. Goodnight, Simon."

Max arrived home very late and looked, to Jane's worried eyes, absolutely dead beat. Having greeted Simon, handing over the gift he had promised—a Red Indian outfit complete with full head dress that Simon seemed to imagine all Americans wore—he took Simon to bed and then came downstairs to Jane. He just put his arms round her, holding her for a very long time without speaking, finally saying in a low, vibrant voice, "I never knew I could miss anyone so much."

"I missed you too."

"I should like to stay here and prove to you how much I've missed you, but, oh, Jane, I'm so tired that not even you could keep me awake much longer." He smiled apologetically and rested his mouth softly on hers. "I'm sorry, my love, but I feel as though I've spent the last fortnight flying round and round the States without ever stopping long enough to get my bearings. Will you be very annoyed if I just go to bed and we do our proper greetings tomorrow?"

"Of course not. You look very tired, Max. Go to bed."

"I wish you could come with me," he said, and then laughed a little self-mockingly. "Even if you did, I wouldn't be much use to you tonight. Goodnight, my darling love. See you in the morning." Jane watched him go and smiled as she picked up his brief case and took it into the library, then hung up his coat. She felt like a wife already.

Eight

The morning brought many things: Simon whooping it up all over the house with his Red Indian outfit on, his face ghoulishly made up with lipstick he had charmed out of Beth; a fresh fall of snow that transformed the pleasant English countryside into something bleakly Arctic like; a present for Jane from Max in the form of a diamond and sapphire engagement ring and . . . the post.

There was no reason why the post should be anything special that morning. Jane usually dealt with it before breakfast but because of the snow, the postman was late and it came mid-morning, when Jane and Max were in the library. Despite their new relationship, there was still a novel to be completed and though Jane had learned to her delight what a passionate lover Max could be, he could also be very practical, not even wanting to take one day off after the harrowing American trip. Much refreshed after a good night's sleep, he was going over some notes he had made while in the States, when Beth brought in the post.

"Leave it here, Beth," Max said. "I'll see to it since Jane is busy."

Jane glanced up at him over her typewriter, watching him sort through the large pile of letters, and their eyes met. They smiled warmly at each other. Then Jane returned to her typing.

"What's this?" Max said a little later. In his hand was what looked like a newspaper or magazine, rolled up so that it could be sent through the post with one of the brown paper labels designed for the purpose. Even then the penny did not immediately drop for Jane. A long time afterwards she was still amazed at how softly and gently a bomb could fall. She watched him rip open the paper wrapper and shake out the magazine. There was a letter accompanying it which Max read aloud. By then Jane's hands were stiff on the typewriter keys and she was aware of blood hammering in her ears. She had caught a glimpse of the cover of the magazine. It was *Looking Glass* and on the front was what looked like the reproduction of an old theatre bill with Max's name upon it.

" 'Dear Mr. Carstairs,' " Max read, " 'Please accept a complimentary copy of *Looking Glass*. I trust you will be satisfied with the feature about you. I am sure you will agree that our special correspondent has done her research thoroughly.' . . . what the hell? It's signed, Alistair Bennett. Never heard of him." He picked up the magazine and looked at the front cover, the frown on his face one of mere puzzlement. Jane watched like one mesmerised; minutes seemed to pass as he turned the pages, his eyes moving slowly over them. For the life of her, Jane could neither move nor speak. Then a sort of shudder went through him and his hands clenched convulsively on the magazine as, with all his pent up fury, he flung it at Jane. "Look!" he shouted. "Look at your hand-iwork!"

Jane caught the magazine and looked at the relevant pages. The headline screamed at her in glaring black letters— "Max Carstairs, the lost star. Where is he now?" and below this, in small letters she read "By our special correspondent, Jane Murray." These words alone did not cause her involuntary gasp of disbelief. The illustrations were the things that made her wonder if it would help if she fainted or just died. There they were, so familiar; Simon and Max standing beside the snowman in the garden; Simon yelling with excitement as he played in the snow; Jane and Max looking into each other's eyes. All these precious photographs, spread all over the magazine for everyone to look at. Jane licked dry lips, lifting her eyes with difficulty to Max. He was still sitting there, staring at her, his face dead white so that the scar throbbed visibly. Jane had never known anyone could look so furious and so wretched at the same time, but she realised at once that in the end anger would dominate the misery.

"Max, I didn't . . . this isn't what you think," she whispered lamely, too shocked and bewildered to explain clearly.

"Really? You mean you don't know this Alistair Bennett?" His voice was beautiful as always, but clipped and cold, shattering her into incoherance, unable to defend herself. Besides, what defence was there? She had no idea how this came about. She had taken those photographs, hadn't she? She had the originals and the negatives; she knew she had been set up by Alistair, but she had no notion how he had laid hands on those photographs.

"Do you know him?" Max asked, his voice steadier now, so that she had the nerve to answer him.

"Yes, but . . ."

"No buts, Jane. Spare me your excuses. My God, how can you look so sweet and innocent, worming your way into Simon's affections, into my . . ."

"It isn't like that!" Jane cried, finding her voice at last, leaping to her feet, desperate to exonerate herself, to get rid of this nightmare. "Max, really it isn't. I didn't give Alistair any of this . . . how he got the photos . . . I don't know . . . believe me. It's true he asked me to—to come here, and at first I agreed to do what he asked but . . ."

"I see," he interrupted, standing with her and walking round his desk so that she backed away, frightened by the blank look in his eyes. This look told her, suddenly and inexorably, that nothing she could say would make any difference. The caged violence that she read there caused her to gasp and cover her mouth with her hand. "You came to spy on me, did you? Christ, what a laugh you must have had, you and this Alistair Bennett. What is he to you? A boyfriend perhaps . . . or more than that?" The tone was so insulting that she flinched.

"No," she said with a little groan of despair. "Max, listen to me, please."

"Listen to you, you bitch? I wouldn't listen to you if you were the last woman on earth. There is no way, no way, that Bennett could have got those photos unless you handed them over. I could kill you for that. I realised I loved you that day—those pictures were something special—or so I thought. How bloody naïve can one man get?" He looked at her with derision, his mouth twisted into a sneer. "Get out," he said. "Get out before I

153

do something I'll regret, like breaking your neck. Get out of this room and out of my house!"

He turned from her and she asked, dully, "How can I go? It's so far to the station and it's snowing."

"Do you think I care how the hell you go?" he demanded, a snarl lurking in his voice so that for the first time tears began to threaten her. "Get a taxi, or a bus, or bloody well walk! I don't care how you go. Just get out!"

She stumbled out of the door, across the hall and up to her room, where she sat on the bed, numbed, unable to think what to do. It was much later that she moved, stiffly, wincing as the blood began to pump through cold, aching limbs. In dull, robot-like movements, she took down her suitcase and began to pack. Then she put on her coat and knee-length, fur lined boots. She picked up her handbag and only then did her brain become alert enough to think about the photographs. She opened the large handbag quickly and scrabbled about, finding the envelope that held the snaps. She stared in dismay and puzzlement; all the negatives were there just as they should be. It didn't make sense, but she was too bewildered and miserable to care just now.

She looked round at the neat little room that had become her home over the last few months and thought how she would miss it and how happy she had been there. She tried not to think of Max—she didn't dare think of him yet—his anger or his misery. Not for one moment did she doubt that he was as unhappy as she was, perhaps even more so, for he believed she had betrayed his love, probably that she had even pretended to love him, whereas she knew that, whatever the truth about the magazine article, the only real truth was that she loved him completely and forever. She tugged off the ring that had adorned her finger a few short hours and left it in its leather box on the dressing table. Then tears threatened again and she bit them back and went downstairs carrying her suitcase. Mrs. Hoskyns came from the kitchen and surveyed her with troubled eyes. She had no doubt heard Max yelling in the library, even if she hadn't heard the actual words.

"Mr. Carstairs told me to order you a taxi, Jane. It should be here in a few minutes."

At least he cared enough to be concerned about her. Jane's heart ached with thankfulness for that. "Thank you, Mrs. Hoskyns. Do you know the train times?"

"There's one at just after one o'clock for London. But with snow, who can tell?"

"Oh, well, I'll just have to wait and see." Jane looked round the hall, remembering the morning when she had tried to run away and Max had stopped her. It would have been better for them all if she had managed to make her escape. Mrs. Hoskyns handed her a carrier bag.

"Some sandwiches, dear, and a flask of coffee. The waiting room is never heated and you'll maybe have a long time to wait for the train. At least it'll help."

Her kindness unravelled Jane as nothing else had; tears rose to her eyes, overspilling before she could stop them. On impulse she flung her arms round the housekeeper's motherly form and kissed her. "Tell Simon goodbye for me," she asked. "I'm sorry I can't see him but . . ."

"I know. Mr. Carstairs asked me to give you this." She gave Jane an envelope. "I suppose it's your wages."

"Yes." Jane was tempted to return the envelope, saying she wanted nothing from him, but she was practical enough to know she would need the money, and besides, she had earned it honestly. "Thank you," she murmured and went out to the waiting taxi.

The taxi took an age to reach the station, crawling through what was little less than a blizzard; already where the land was open and unsheltered, the snow had piled into drifts, and though the main roads were being kept clear by snow ploughs, the side roads were treacherous. Occasionally Jane caught glimpses of groups of forest ponies huddled together, their backs to the driving wind. When she went into the station, the station master told her the line was blocked to the south and it might be some time before a train got through. Jane was past caring. She sat in the cold waiting room and after a little while ate the sandwiches Mrs. Hoskyns had given her, and drank some of the coffee. Her watch told her she had already been there an hour.

It had been quiet in the small station but now there was a commotion outside. Jane heard loud male voices and as she turned her head to listen, the door was flung open and Max came in, bringing with him a flurry of snow and freezing air. He was wearing his duffel coat and snow lay thickly upon it and on his hair as though he had been outside some time. Jane stared at him, noting the deathly pallor of his face, whiteness that went clear to his lips, too surprised at his sudden appearance to do more than stare. Before she even had time to be happy at the thought that he had come after her, he said harshly, "Have you seen Simon?"

She gazed stupidly at him, open-mouthed and

not understanding. Then she shook her head. "Simon? Of course not. He's not here."

Max's shoulders slumped and he seemed to shrink visibly. He rubbed his wet hair in a distraught fashion and muttered, "I didn't think so really . . . he couldn't have got so far. It was just a vain hope."

Jane was on her feet now, forgetting everything but the surge of fear that shot through her. She rushed over to him. "Max, what is this? What's happened?"

He shook his head uncertainly, seemingly trying to put his words into a semblance of order. "He disappeared . . . left a note saying he was going to look for you . . . he must have heard . . . oh, Christ, I don't know . . . I must go and look . . ." He turned away rather blindly and she clutched his arm.

"The police . . . have you called the police?"

"Of course. Hours ago. It seems like hours anyway."

Somewhere far off a telephone rang and he raised his head, listening. A moment later the station master appeared. "It's for you, Mr. Carstairs," he called, and Max was gone, heading for the office before the man had finished speaking. Jane heard his voice, harsh and urgent, and then a broken cry of anguish. "Oh, thank God!"

"He's been found," she whispered to Max when he reappeared. He looked whiter than ever now and merely nodded, before saying, curtly, "You'd better come with me."

"What?"

"For Christ's sake, it's all your damn fault anyway!" he shouted at her. "The least you can do is come back and satisfy him that you haven't gone off without saying goodbye to him."

Jane made no comment on the injustice of this attack. He was desperately worried and it didn't bother her if he chose to expiate his own guilt by increasing hers. Perhaps really they were both to blame. She collected her things and followed him out to his car. The drive back to Mill House was frightening. Conditions were much worse than when she had come down in the taxi and Max drove fast, too fast, hunched forward over the steering wheel and giving no thought to the safety of himself or his passenger. When they reached the house, he went inside, leaving Jane to follow with her own luggage. She was met in the hall by Mrs. Hoskyns who told her in a low voice that Simon had been found about half a mile away.

"He was in a state of collapse, poor mite, and it was pure luck that the policeman saw him. The doctor's sent for an ambulance."

In the end Simon, unconscious and half-dead from exposure, was driven through the snow to the hospital where he lay like a little broken doll in an oxygen tent. For four days Max sat like a gaunt shadow beside the bed, his eyes scarcely leaving his son's face. Jane stayed some of the time with him, sometimes managing to persuade him to rest though never for long, pushing cups of coffee and sandwiches into his hands. She doubted if he even knew she was there.

At last the double pneumonia loosed its grip and Simon was taken home. Max hired a private nurse who ruled the sick room with a hand of iron, refusing admittance to everyone except Max. Jane hung about the house, listless and disturbed, in a kind of limbo. She was grateful for the kindness and friendship of the staff for Max seldom spoke to her. Obviously he hadn't forgiven her for what he thought of as her duplicity. Until now he had been too concerned about Simon to think about her, but now she began to feel the force of his hatred and his resentment at having to put up with her for Simon's sake.

Simon had been out of hospital several days when Max came into the morning room where Jane was staring gloomily into a cup of coffee, and told her Simon wanted to see her. These were the first civilised words Max had spoken to her for some time and Jane looked hopefully at him, but his facial expression was bleak and unyielding. She sighed and stood up.

"Should I go now?" she asked, and he nodded.

The door to Simon's room was opened by the nurse, a Mrs. Kitty O'Brian, who was in uniform. She was in her late thirties, and looked kind, friendly and uncomplicated, greeting Jane with a hearty handshake. "Good of you to come so promptly, my dear," she said with a faint Liverpudlian accent. "Simon, me lad, look who's here to see you."

Simon's response was both gratifying and heart-rending. He clung round Jane's neck, his face pressed into her shoulder. He felt so thin, without any real substance, that Jane could have cried for him. She swallowed down the sobs convulsively and said lightly, "Well now, Simon, what have you been doing to yourself?"

"I've been very ill," he said importantly. "Did you know I've been very, very ill?"

Jane laughed. Despite his pale little face and huge eyes, he was still the same Simon. "Yes, I knew. I also know that you're getting better all the time."

"Well, I do feel sort of better, specially now you're here, Jane." He held on tightly to her as he laid back on the pillow, looking exhausted from the exertion of greeting her. "I went out to look for you, out in the snow, 'cos I heard you tell Mrs. Hoskyns you were going away. An' you didn't say goodbye. You won't go away again, will you, Jane?"

"No, darling, I won't. At least not till you're completely better."

"Promise," he pleaded and she nodded and promised. It was a promise that was easy to make but which proved to be very, very difficult to keep.

Jane had hoped at first that Philip might appear to lend her a little moral support, but Philip was in Europe doing some research for Max. Jane seldom saw Max, which was a relief because when she did see him he was so cold and hate-filled that their meetings left her feeling weak and shaken. Nothing was ever mentioned about the article in *Looking Glass* but Jane sensed that Max's fury had not abated with time. Were it not for Simon and the promise she had made him, she would never have stayed. But though his recovery would have continued in a slow but sure pace without her presence, Kitty told her bluntly that he might fall back were she to leave.

"He loves you like a mother," she told Jane. "The mother he never had, poor lad. No, Jane, if you want the truth of the matter, it would be as well for the boy if you stayed till he's fit."

"When will that be?" Jane asked in a low voice, knowing she had to get away from Max before she could begin the long, painful process of getting over her love for him.

"Let's say another couple of months."

* * *

Eight more weeks! Eight weeks of being slowly torn apart! Jane shuddered at the thought as she went downstairs, intending to go out for some fresh air. It was a blue-skied day and the sun was quite warm. She flung a jacket across her shoulders and set off across the lawns, breathing the fresh air as though she had been deprived of it for too long. The atmosphere of Mill House, that she had once loved so much, now stifled and restricted her so that it was a relief to get outside. How different things might have been, she thought sadly, if the article hadn't been printed. She would have been married to Max by now and all this glory would have been hers.

"Oh, no!" she gasped almost with physical pain, and knew she must never think of these "if onlys."

She stopped walking, noting that her feet had led her to the rose garden. Some of the roses were beginning to support new shoots and leaves, but they were so neglected that she doubted if there would be much of a show. She sighed and leaned on the little gate, so lost in thought that she did not hear Max approaching until he was just a few yards away, and then she jumped in surprise and alarm, looking at him with unhappy defiance.

"Trespassing again?" he drawled softly, his words and their connotation sending prickles of unease down Jane's spine.

"I don't think so. Did you want something?"

A sort of smile lurked round his mouth, a smile more contemptuous than humorous, and his eyes moved slowly over her body, in a way that caused her apprehension to increase. "Did I want something?" he murmured. "Maybe I did. You've improved, Jane, over the last few weeks. You've got thin but it suits you. I would say that you are almost beautiful."

"I don't want compliments from you!" Jane said tartly, going to walk past him. She was brought up short as his hand shot out and grabbed her wrist, pulling her round to face him.

"Don't walk away when I'm talking to you!" he said tersely.

"We haven't anything to say to each other," she said. "You have made it abundantly clear what you think of me."

"Maybe. But there are things for a man and woman to do other than talking."

Her eyes dilated and darkened with fear. "What do you mean? Let me go, you're hurting my arm."

He smiled at her, the sort of smile she imagined a tiger might give before it ate its victim, a smile that held a hint of cruelty she had always suspected might be hidden in him somewhere. Then he drew her slowly to him, his hands sliding down her back to her hips, pressing her hard against his body. Until then she had stayed still, looking mesmerised into his eyes, but now she realised what was happening and stiffened, putting her hands against his chest and pushing at him.

"What are you doing? Leave me alone!"

She might as well have saved her strength. He completely ignored her feeble attempts to evade his embrace. While one arm tightened round her, holding her hard, the other hand dug into her hair, pulling cruelly at it so that her head was forced back and she cried out in pain. Her cries were cut off by his mouth on hers—a hard, angry mouth that fastened relentlessly on hers, remorseless as the man himself. For one awful moment the world swung round her and she thought she would pass out, then the pressure eased so that she was able to draw a shuddering breath. His lips moved to the curve of her throat and he said her name, his voice husky with desire.

"Let me go!" she cried, still trying to struggle within the iron clamps that were his arms. "Please, Max, let me go!"

"Let you go! Never!" He looked into her pleading eyes, his smile alight with triumph as he took her mouth again, forcing her lips open. "You still love me, Jane. Admit it, then I might let you go—for a little while anyway."

"No I don't!" she shouted. "I hate you!"

He kissed her once more, and then again and again, until she hung limp in his arms, unable to think or to feel, while tears ran unheeded down her face. Then suddenly he was holding her more gently, kissing away the tears, stroking her hair, exploring the tender curves of her neck and shoulders with sensitive lips, and her body stirred in his arms as she struggled, no longer against him but against herself and the urge to respond. He seemed to sense this inner turmoil for his hands caressed her, bringing her to life.

"You know you still love me, Jane. Admit it. Tell me," he ordered.

"No," she murmured. Her mouth trembled against his, her eyes closed against his insistent lips and she began to return his kisses because she could no longer help herself, her arms slipping round his neck. "Oh, Max, I love you," she moaned. "I love you."

Immediately she was released and her eyes flew open as she gazed uncertainly at him. He looked straight into her eyes, a contemptuous curve on his mouth. "Good. That's what I wanted to hear."

163

"Wh . . . what do you mean?" she whispered.

"What do you think I mean?" he demanded, the contempt more marked now. "I want you to know how it feels to have your love thrust back in your teeth. It's not pleasant, is it, Jane?"

She shook her head, bewildered. "You can't . . . I don't understand."

"Don't you? You will before long," he said grimly. "By the time I've finished with you, you'll wish you had never been born."

Jane shuddered at the low-pitched ferocity in his voice. She understood now, oh yes, indeed she understood. He must all this time have been wondering how to wreak his vengeance upon her and now had punished her more cruelly than he could possibly know, forcing her to admit her love for him and then flinging it back unwanted. She longed to cry out with her pain and despair but would not give way before him. His bitterness stemmed from what he believed she had done to him, and in a twisted way, his punishment was a form of justice—or would have been had she been guilty. She looked into his implacable face. God! How she must have hurt him!

"I'll leave," she managed to whisper. "I'll leave at once."

"Oh, no, my girl, you're not getting off that lightly. You aren't going anywhere."

"How do you intend stopping me? You can't keep me prisoner!"

"Don't put ideas into my head," he said dryly. "I was thinking of Simon. You promised him you would stay, didn't you?"

Jane flushed, more angry now than hurt. "How can you be so low? To use a sick little boy just to get your own petty revenge!"

His face took on a ferocious look; she saw that

his hands had clenched into fists and his jaw tightened. He took a step forward. "You suggest that again and you'll be very sorry!"

"Really? What would you do?" she flashed back, blinking away sudden tears. "Beat me?"

"Oh no, my sweet." His voice dropped dramatically and his cold eyes roamed over her body, taking in every detail of her, lingering thoughtfully on the soft curves of her breast beneath the thin silk shirt she wore. She swiftly drew her coat round her, and the movement caused him to laugh. "The punishment would be much more delightful than that."

If he *had* beaten her, he couldn't have hurt her more. Jane flinched visibly and paled, saying in a low gulping voice, "How can you be so cruel?"

"I had a good teacher."

"That's not true!" she cried. "I never betrayed you. If you really loved me you would have believed me. I never gave that information to Alistair! I know that's why I came here at first but I had already told him that I couldn't do it."

"You lie most convincingly, my darling. And what about the photographs? How can you explain that? My God, you must think me stupid, or too blindly in love, to think straight. Well, blind I was but no more. There's no explanation you can give that I would believe."

"I haven't got an explanation to give because I don't know how Alistair got the pictures. I tried to phone him to find out but he wouldn't speak to me." Her voice trembled and for a brief, hopeful moment he looked puzzled as though he had doubts. But then he shook his head.

"No. There's no way out. You're a liar and a cheat, and by God, I intend to make you suffer!"

"I'll leave," she whispered. "I will."

"No you won't. Not as long as Simon is ill, because if you broke your promise to him I think I really would kill you. The doctor reckons he'll be completely well in a couple of months and that's long enough. I wouldn't have even you wriggling on a pin longer than that."

"I hate you!" she shouted, her voice heavy with distress. "I hate you!"

"No you don't. You love me. You said so a few minutes ago, very sweetly too, as you lay so limply in my arms. Why, I believe it would be easy to arouse that emotion in you again." He took a step forward and she, in a panic, stepped back, coming up hard against the gate. He reached out for her, his eyes without expression now, and as his hands closed on her shoulders, one large tear overspilled and ran down her cheek. She turned her face away and he dropped his hands, stepping back.

"Tears! How touching. I suppose I should now melt before them, take you in my arms and beg your pardon. Say that I don't care what you've done so long as we can be together. Strangely enough, if you had admitted it, I would have forgiven you. There wasn't much wrong with that article—at least it was truthful. It's the deceit, the underhandedness I can't stand, and your continual professions of innocence. If you would only tell the truth . . ."

"I have told the truth! Do you expect me to confess to something I didn't do?" She clapped her hands over her ears and sobbed, "Oh, go away! Go away and leave me alone! I can't stand anymore of this!" She closed her eyes and turned away from him, and in a moment he walked away. Only then did the full pain creep over her and she leaned against the gate, bent over almost double as the sobs which she had for so long held back, broke out and she cried as though her heart really could break.

Nine

Simon was getting better now and was allowed up for three or four hours every day. He was allowed to sit by the fire in his room in his dressing gown, and after tea, Max carried him down to the lounge for an hour so that he could watch children's programmes on the colour television set. During the day time it took all Kitty's and Jane's ingenuity to find things to occupy his mind and keep him from becoming restless.

"He's much better today," Max remarked to Jane one evening, when Simon had finally fallen asleep exhausted after a game with his soldiers.

"Yes, he is," she agreed softly, walking out of the door that Max held open. He closed the door on Simon and Kitty and reached out to Jane, encircling her wrist with strong, taut fingers. It was dark on the upstairs corridor and she remained still, not looking at him; awareness of his height, the latent strength of his fingers, his virility and the clean masculine smell of him, seeped into her and her stomach gripped with a mixture of delight and fear. It was strange that she could hate him so much yet at the same time love him with every fibre of her being.

"You will soon be able to leave me, Jane," he murmured softly.

"The sooner the better," she muttered flatly, not daring to pull away from him. If she did she knew what would happen. It had happened before, when she had tried to escape from him and had found herself being held tightly in his arms while he took his fill of kisses and she stood there unable to move.

Now he came closer and she felt his fingers on her hair. She jerked a little and felt his fingers tighten on her wrist. "Jane," he said, "Come here."

"Leave me alone," she whispered, terribly aware of the closed door behind her and Kitty and Simon just beyond it. "Oh, please."

"Please," he repeated with relish. "How I enjoy hearing you plead." He tipped her chin up and found her mouth with his, his lips soft and sensual as they explored her face. Jane's head swam as she willed herself not to give him the satisfaction of feeling her response. Yet she knew it was only a matter of time before her stupid, weak body, which seemed to be no part of her where he was concerned, gave way to his insistent, experienced caresses. And as always, the moment her resolve collapsed, her mouth trembled into response, her arms went round him, he released her, leaving her shaking with emptiness and loss.

"Haven't you had enough?" she gulped. "Can't you leave me alone?"

"You still love me, Jane. How touching that despite the way I treat you, you still love me. How long, I wonder, before you begin to hate me."

She looked up at him gravely, her eyes reproachful. "Do you want me to hate you, Max?"

she asked softly, her voice breaking, and she was sure she saw some kind of anguish flash through his eyes before she turned from him and ran away along the carpeted corridor.

On the following Saturday morning, knowing that Max was with Simon, Jane went into the library. She often did this when she was sure she would not be surprised in there by Max. Here, in this lovely room, she could relax and forget the torture of her present life, remembering only happy things. In this room she could even forgive Max for what he was doing to her and understand a little of why he was doing it. He had been hurt, very, very hurt, and was striking back because it was the only way to lessen the pain. And though what he believed was untrue, this did not make that pain any less.

Jane looked round the room. It was very tidy and neat; the desk that had been hers was bare except for the covered typewriter. Max had not found himself another secretary. As far as she knew, he had stopped writing altogether. She went across to his desk, opening a loose-leaf file and looking through the notes in his handwriting that it contained. She didn't care that she was prying into what didn't concern her. There was nothing worse he could do to her even if he discovered her.

Max's handwriting was not easy to read. He wrote swiftly to keep up with his thoughts and sometimes, when called on to make typewritten copies of his notes she had difficulty reading his scrawl. The notes were about his American trip, a kind of résumé of the lectures he had given, the people he had met, the places visited. In a little while her eye got in again so that she was able to read more easily. It was fascinating stuff written in his usual succinct, sometimes hilariously funny and always entertaining style; she sank down on to his chair. She was immersed in a beautiful, though chilling description of Death Valley in California, when the door opened and Max himself came in.

"What the hell are you doing?" he demanded peremptorily.

Jane looked mildly at him, determined not to be intimidated, meeting his stormy gaze with equanimity. "I suppose you would say I'm poking my nose in where it doesn't belong."

Something that was almost a smile touched his hard mouth. There was certainly a lightening of his expression. Impulsively her heart warmed with love for him though she knew she should have more sense. She said, "I'll type these notes if you like."

"No thank you," he said stiffly. "I don't doubt that when Simon is better and I can get back to work, I'll get another secretary."

"Oh! Yes, of course." Swiftly Jane closed the file and stood up, anxious now only to get out without precipitating another scene with him. She heard the sound of a car engine which drew her eyes to the window, and she watched Margot Copeland getting out of her blue Rover.

"It's Mrs. Copeland," she said unnecessarily.

"So I see."

"I'll . . . I'll tell her you're in here, shall I?"

"Thank you."

As Jane walked into the hall, she came face to face with Margot, who had let herself in with her own key. The two women looked at each other, the ready smile on Jane's face fading into bafflement as she saw the expression on Margot's. It began as surprise, then annoyance and finally a fury so wild that it was almost maniacal. Then, even as Jane opened her mouth to speak, Margot strode past her, pushing her hard against the wall, and marched into the library, flinging the door open with considerable force. Jane heard just a few words before the door was slammed shut again.

"Max, what in the name of God is that girl doing here still? After all the trouble I . . ."

Jane pulled a face and rubbed her arm which tingled from the collision with the wall. Something strange was going on and without thinking why, she sat on the bottom stair listening to the sounds coming from within the library. She could not make out any separate words but there was certainly a lot of shouting going on and once Max's voice rose in a loud, furious and disbelieving shout. Soon after this he came out of the room and looked at Jane. He seemed rather pale and shaken while his chest heaved as though he were under some considerable pressure.

"Would you mind coming in please, Jane?" he asked in a quiet and polite voice, and stood back so that she could walk past him. Margot was sitting by the fire, sobbing in a distracted, unrestrained way that contrasted very much with her coolly controlled appearance. "Jane," Max said from behind her, coming in and closing the door, "Margot has something to tell you. Will you sit down?"

"I'd rather stand," she told him and he nodded.

"As you like. Margot, we are waiting."

"I can't!" she sobbed. "I can't!"

"Yes you can. By God, you'd better. Everything. Now!"

She was still so upset that she could hardly speak and Jane glanced reproachfully at Max who was so implacable. He went to the drinks trolley and came back with a large brandy which he thrust into the distraught woman's hand. She gulped the liquid down in one swallow.

"Now," he said with no compassion in his voice. "From the beginning."

"All right . . . all right." Margot looked at Jane, her expression resentful despite her distress. "I . . . I knew that Max was attracted to you and I wanted to put a stop to it. It was I whom Max should marry . . . me! Not some stupid little fool scarcely out of school. But I didn't know what to do. I tried warning you off but that didn't work." She sniffed in an angry sort of way but now she had begun she seemed quite willing to continue. "Then I saw Alistair Bennett in the village. I knew him years ago and wondered what he was doing down here. But he acted very mysterious—he mentioned you and I told him how I disliked you and that you were throwing yourself at Max. Then just after Christmas, he got in touch with me in London. He told me everything about how you had let him down. I knew by then that you were going to marry Max and it seemed the perfect opportunity to get rid of you. Alistair and I got together and worked out how we could both use the situation to our advantage. So I . . ." She halted and glanced at Max who was glaring at her as he had never, even at his fiercest, glared at Jane. "I gave him all the information and I got the photographs. I took the negatives from your room one day—it was when Max was in the States and you were out with Simon. I got them to Alistair who had prints taken from them at once, and I was able to return the negatives without you having even missed them."

In the silence that followed, broken only by

renewed sobs from Margot, Jane sat down, unable to take her own weight any longer, unable to look at Max, unable to think of anything except this woman who had systematically set her up, ruining hers and Max's chance of happiness.

"That's all," Margot sobbed. "Can I go now?"

"I think that might be a good idea," Max said bleakly.

In the library there was silence. Not a sound permeated the room save her own uneven breathing and his. Jane stared at the carpet and tried to think coherently. She felt no hostility towards Margot; if anyone was to blame it was Alistair who had so cold-bloodedly used a neurotic woman for his own ends.

"What can I say?" Max's voice was like a whisper that ran softly round the room before finally reaching her ears.

"Nothing. There's nothing you can say." How weary she sounded, unutterably tired and defenceless and without emotion! She stood up and walked to the door, still not looking at him. He reached the door before her, asking in a low voice, "Where are you going? What will you do?"

"I . . . don't know. I can't think. Leave me alone, please."

"Yes . . . after what has happened I have no right . . ." he hesitated, his hand on her arm and she at last raised her eyes and looked into his. He looked very, very old. "Just one thing, don't just go . . . I mean, stay until you've got yourself sorted out. I won't force my presence on you . . ." His mouth twisted with bitterness against himself. "God knows I've done enough of that."

"It doesn't matter. But I think I should go."

"I see." There was such a heaviness in him, in his voice, his eyes, in the weight of his hand on her arm, that she added gently, "I think it would be best, for everyone."

"Best? If it's best for you, if you feel that after the past weeks you can't bear to stay a moment longer with me—and God knows, I wouldn't blame you—then I understand that. But don't go because it's best for me. It isn't . . . I can't think of anything worse."

She looked steadily at him, then she said, "This time I won't go without saying goodbye to Simon," and slipped out of the door which he held open.

Once when she had been feeling particularly low and desperate to talk to someone, Jane had confided in Kitty the whole of the story of her relationship with Max. Now, as she went along to her room to pack, Kitty followed her and stood in the doorway. Jane told her, in a stilted voice that still shook from reaction, what Margot had done. "I'll say goodbye to Simon," she added. "When he wakes up."

"Aye, you're going to punish him then?"

"Simon?" Jane asked, startled.

"No, Mr. Carstairs I mean. You want to punish him for what he did to you. Well, it's only natural I suppose."

"No!" Jane cried horrified. "It isn't that. Never!"

"Then why are you leaving? Have you stopped loving him, child? Did he finally make you hate him as he set out to do?"

"No."

"By leaving like this, you'll be making all three of you miserable. You, the boss, and the lad." Kitty came into the room, going right up to Jane, her usually placid face alight with determination and a pleading look. "Don't ruin your life for what's no more than a foolish principle, Jane. I know, believe me, I know. There's no pride in love."

Jane stared at her, and suddenly it all clicked into place, as though she had found the last piece of a very difficult jigsaw puzzle. "You're right, Kitty," she whispered, hugging her. "Oh, thank you for making me see sense before it was too late." Kitty grinned faintly as she watched the girl running along the corridor and down the stairs to the library.

Max was at his desk, his head in his hands, utter despair written in every line of his body. When Jane entered, softly closing the door behind her, he looked up slowly, fixing his eyes upon her.

"Max . . . I've decided I'll stay after all."

"You've seen Simon then?" he inquired softly and she shook her head.

"He's still asleep. If you want me still . . . I'll stay with . . . with you."

There was a long, painful silence while he stared at her, his face working in an agony of uncertainty, and then he had covered the distance between them, pulling her into his arms, crushing her to him and kissing her, saying her name over and over again.

"Jane," he groaned into her hair. "I can't apologise for hurting you so badly, because there are no words, and I'm sure that you must know. If it's any consolation, every time I hurt you, I was only turning the screw on my own misery. Oh, God! How could I have been such a fool? How can you forgive me? Jane! You do forgive me?"

"There's nothing to forgive, not now." She lifted her tear-streaked face to his. "Cry if you want to," he said with rough tenderness. "I won't ever make you cry again, I promise you that. You have only to say the word and I would willingly spend the rest of my life making up these weeks to you."

"I don't know what the word is," she said simply, smiling at him through her tears. "Will it do just to say I love you?"

"Will it do?" he echoed huskily. "Oh, God, my darling Jane, how it will do!"

ABOUT THE AUTHOR

Anne Neville lives with her husband in the beautiful cathedral town of Salisbury in Wiltshire, England— and teaches primary school in a small village nearby. She has published ten contemporary romances and also writes historical novels under the name Jane Viney. Her favorite ways of relaxing are horseback riding, dressmaking and embroidery.

CIRCLE OF LOVE

Step out of your world and enter the Circle of Love.

Six new CIRCLE OF LOVE romances are available every month. Here's a preview of the six newest titles on sale May 15, 1982:

#16 INNOCENT DECEPTION by Anne Neville (#21516-7 • $1.75)

It was a chance for Laurel to taste a life of unaccustomed luxury. But little did she realize the consequences of impersonating her glamorous, coldhearted twin sister—or how her own heart would betray her once she was thrust into the arms of Derek Clayton, her sister's estranged but wealthy husband.

#17 PAMELA by Mary Mackie (#21505-1 • $1.75)

Pamela woke in a hospital room with no memory of her past, no knowledge of her name. Her only thought was of her instant attraction to the hostile and handsome man before her. Pamela did not recall anything he told her of her past… and even worse, she felt herself plunging headlong into careless desire for this dangerously seductive man.

#18 SAND CASTLES by Alexandra Kirk (#21529-9 • $1.75)

Jason Kent always got what he wanted. And now he wanted Melissa to give up her independence and become governess to his young, motherless daughter. But could she cope with the desires which welled up in her heart when Jason was near? And could she stand to be so close to him—and watch him marry another woman?

CIRCLE OF LOVE

O

With Circle of Love Romances, you treat yourself to a romantic holiday—anytime, anywhere. Enter The Circle of Love—and travel to faraway places with romantic heroes....

21502	GOLD IN HER HAIR	$1.75
21507	ROYAL WEDDING	$1.75
21500	DESIGN FOR ENCHANTMENT	$1.75
21510	THE HEATHER IS WINDBLOWN	$1.75
21508	GATES OF THE SUN	$1.75
21509	A RING AT THE READY	$1.75
21506	ASHTON'S FOLLY	$1.75
21504	THE RELUCTANT DAWN	$1.75
21503	THE CINDERELLA SEASON	$1.75